all i knead for christmas

Walleye Point Small-Town Romance

alison stone

ALL I KNEAD FOR CHRISTMAS is available in ebook and print:

Ebook ISBN: 978-1-964598-09-3

Print ISBN: 978-1-964598-10-9

*

---

*   23Jun25

1 /
emily

"It's December. Not sure why they can't wait." Talking hands-free to my friend back home in Pittsburgh, I drummed my fingers on the steering wheel, impatience thrumming through me. Working late most nights meant I usually avoided the after-school traffic, but not this time. The Walleye Point School District clearly had no interest in efficiency. Every time I thought the school bus was *finally* on its way, its brake lights flared red again, the safety arm swinging out like some smug meddler pointing to the back of the line.

"Why would you risk it?" he said. "And this is coming from a guy who gave up late nights at the office for a mortgage, a minivan, and a toddler who negotiates like a Wall Street shark at bedtime." Dylan's voice sounded exasperated through the phone but laced with that dry humor that made endless banking hours bearable. We both knew all the sacrifices of late nights, strategic job pivots, and a constant grind. That was what all of it had been for. And yet, there I was, risking it all by leaving Pittsburgh and driving the two hours north to Walleye Point.

"You don't drive a minivan." I tracked the two kids who got off at this stop and ran up the long driveway to a well-maintained Victorian home just beyond the center of town. Black smoke puffed from the bus's exhaust pipe in the frigid afternoon. The bus made it three more houses before the red lights flashed, and the safety arm swung out. *Again.* I tilted my head back and forth, trying to ease the tension in my neck. The inclement weather and news of my sister's accident had wound all my muscles tight.

"You get my point."

"You're talking to me like I don't already know that." I released a long breath, trying to calm the butterflies fluttering in my belly. I was looking to him for reassurance. Returning to Walleye Point hadn't come at a convenient time. *Is there such a thing?*

A young teenage girl hopped out of the bus at the next stop, her long brown ponytail swinging back and forth. Reflexively, I touched my hair. It flowed over the collar of my black winter coat, which was more dressy than functional. I didn't think my hair had ever been that thick. Ponytail Girl stopped at the end of her drive and spun around to give a quick wave to her friends still on the bus. Only after it pulled away did the teen turn on the heel of her boot and run up the driveway. Something about her body language suggested she was one of the popular ones. Not the kind who got off the bus with a full backpack and worries weighing on her. I eased off the brake and pressed my lips together, willing the bus to go, go, go.

"The holidays are the busiest time for the bakery." I pressed on, as Dylan had failed to provide the definitive reassurance I was looking for. "My sister will lose her shirt at the bakery without me. Blue Moon will still be there in January."

But will your job offer?

A rush of goose bumps raced across my skin. Tempting fate with my own overconfidence was essentially begging karma to strike me down.

"Why are you making me stress about this?" I shifted

again, trying to work out the kink in my thigh. I hadn't dared activate cruise control on slick I-79 or the New York State Thruway, the most direct routes between my cute apartment in Pittsburgh and the small town where I had spent summers with my grandmother.

"*You* brought it up," he said. I could imagine Dylan reclining in his leather chair, hands clasped behind his head, gearing up for the inevitable *I told you so* when this all went sideways. But that was my insecure, second-guessing inner teenager talking, not the confident financial pro who negotiated top salaries, snagged bonuses, and landed plum jobs. And Dylan knew that. He'd always enjoyed messing with me. It started back in college and picked up again when we ended up working at the same firm. The one I'd just resigned from. We'd spent years trading jabs and one-upping each other on the slippery rungs of the corporate ladder.

And we were both killing it.

Blue Moon Investment Group would be foolish to pass me up. I'd survived multiple rounds of interviews and crushed case studies. Their feedback had been one of overwhelming enthusiasm with cheery proclamations about how sharp I was and how well I'd fit in with their team. The hiring manager, Lance Quinn, had even encouraged me to take care of family first, because *that* was what they were all about. Hopefully, he meant it.

"You're right, I did bring it up." My tone softened. I was looking for reassurance, and Dylan knew that. But we were too close for him to feed me a line. Instead, he was doing what he did best, reminding me that Blue Moon Investment Group was *the* job. The reason for all the long hours, the strategic pivots, the sacrifices.

It was the reality check I needed. Help Sammie. Then get back to Pittsburgh to start the job the first full week of the new year. They'd wait. They'd invested too much in me already. All I was waiting for was the formal offer letter.

A tingle of unease crawled up my spine, or maybe it was just another cramp from the long drive. I shifted in my seat, tapping my fingers against the steering wheel as the safety arm folded against the bus. The vehicle lurched forward, back tires spinning briefly on a patch of ice. I adjusted the wipers, clearing the fat snowflakes from my windshield.

I wasn't exactly thrilled to be back in Walleye Point, but at least I'd beaten the worst of the storm. I'd hit the road the minute I cleared out my office. I'd take the win.

"I usually am right," Dylan said smugly. "That's why you called me."

"Again. Not helping." I glanced at the clock on my dash. How was it already this late? "Shouldn't you be picking up that sweet little baby of yours from daycare?" My words were sincere but also a well-aimed shot across the bow. We both knew young kids weren't exactly considered career rocket fuel, especially for women, but also for involved fathers like Dylan. It was one of the sad truths of our industry.

However, once I met baby Victoria, I suddenly got it. Some things were worth the risk.

Family was important. Although, if I was the betting kind, mine wasn't going to be overly thrilled that I was rolling up unannounced. Sammie preferred that I remain the silent partner. I only learned about her broken wrist and severely sprained ankle from my niece, Maddie.

"That sweet little girl is definitely going to derail my career trajectory," Dylan said, his laugh booming through the phone, equal parts amused and resigned.

She had to be—what? Eight or nine months?

"Maybe you shouldn't have married someone just as ambitious as you," I said, teasing and relieved the conversation had shifted away from *my* life choices.

"Ha." He huffed. "Can't help who you fall in love with."

"I'll take your word for it." My career hadn't exactly left room for dating, let alone falling in love. Not that I minded.

Independence had always been my goal. My single mother drilled that lesson into mine and my sister's heads, and with no father around to challenge it, the message stuck. For me anyway. I bit my lip and flicked the wipers up a notch as the snow picked up.

The school bus rolled into town, passing a small park that reminded me of something straight out of *Gilmore Girls*, or maybe just a half-buried memory I wasn't quite ready to dust off.

Dylan kept chatting about baby Victoria's latest milestones, and I responded with the appropriate noises at the right moments, my mind only half on the conversation. Our two-vehicle parade eased through the slippery intersection, marked by the town's one and only flashing red light. As we approached the bakery once belonging to my grandmother, Cookie, I scanned the street for parking and tucked my chin in surprise. Nearly every space was full. So, Sammie hadn't been exaggerating about Walleye Point's so-called resurgence.

The bus's brake lights flared again, and for a second, the place almost felt unfamiliar. The buildings flanking the bakery had undergone an impressive transformation with fresh paint and new signage—a level of upkeep I wasn't expecting. Then I spotted the red-brick storefront, and a knot pulled tight in my stomach. That used to be Mrs. Davis's flower shop. The quaint clapboard siding was gone, bulldozed to make way for the bar's expansion. Irritation simmered in my chest. Those same owners tried to muscle out the bakery too.

But I hadn't let that happen.

My attention turned to the bus just as a handful of kids spilled out, backpacks bouncing, winter hats pulled low over their ears.

"I've arrived at my destination," I said in my best GPS voice. "Parking looks like a disaster. You'd think it was summer with how packed it is."

"Maybe your sister's bakery is doing better than you thought."

"Or maybe the brewery next door is hogging all the spaces," I grumbled.

"Bah, humbug," Dylan said. "Look who's full of holiday cheer."

He had a point. "I gotta go," I said. "Thanks for letting me vent."

"Don't forget what I said. Blue Moon's a top-tier firm. This could be everything you've worked for. Don't—"

"I know." I sagged back in the seat, my nerves shot. "And give that little career wrecker a big squeeze from me."

"You're just jealous, Auntie Emily, because I get all the baby cuddles," Dylan said. Then his voice softened. "Seriously though, don't be a stranger."

"I won't." I ended the call and dragged a hand through my hair, debating if I should go around the block, when the reverse lights of a truck popped on in one of the parking spots in front of the brewery. I tapped my horn to prevent him from putting a huge dent in my car. That was all I needed. A quick check of my rearview allowed me to back up and give him room to back out. Once parked, I finally let my shoulders fall from my ears. I had been one major stress ball since getting that text about Sammie's accident last night.

The wipers gave one final swipe before I turned off the ignition. Two students who had gotten off the bus lingered outside the bakery. My heart leapt. I hadn't realized it before, but the one in the pink Sabres hat was my niece, Maddie. Big white snowflakes fell and melted on my still-warm windshield. My sixteen-year-old niece seemed unfazed by the storm swirling around her. Her winter coat hung open, revealing a bare midriff. I shuddered. I wasn't sure I was ever young enough to be that oblivious to the cold.

The boy acted like he wasn't cold. His green hoodie and matching sweatpants were stamped with the high school's mascot, a cartoon walleye leaping from the water, mouth agape, under the word "Lakers" in bold. With the easy confidence of someone who knew exactly where he stood in the high school food chain, he slouched just enough to make me not want to like him. It wasn't the boy, exactly. It was the memory of every smug jock who'd ever scoffed at me when I raised my hand in class.

Beside him, Maddie threw her head back in laughter. That soft, round face of hers—so much like Sammie's at that age—glowed with happiness. I reached for my purse and started rummaging like I'd lost something, though what I really needed was to lose the feeling that I'd just intruded on a moment I wasn't meant to see.

I hadn't meant to spy. Not really. I had just happened to arrive at this exact time.

When I looked up, they were gone. I climbed out, and a cold breeze hit my neck. I clutched the collar of my coat closed, and a shudder raced up my spine. *Ugh.* Growing up in Buffalo and then moving to Pittsburgh meant I was used to the cold. Didn't mean I liked it.

I reached back into the car, grabbed my cell phone from the holder, and dropped it into my purse. I glanced up, disoriented for a second. I was well aware that the old hole-in-the-wall where I had tried, unsuccessfully, to buy my first beer over ten years ago as an underage teen had reinvented itself as a newfangled brewery, the kind that were also popping up all over Pittsburgh. The brick work and windows gave the business a very modern vibe that required the Walleye Point Bar to be rechristened as Top Shelf Brewery.

I wasn't much of a hockey fan, but I got the pun. In contrast, the word "Bakery" in blue block letters seemed anticlimactic above my grandmother's—well, my sister's—store. They had discussed new signage, but putting out fires had taken priority.

"Lost?"

I squinted against the swirling snow. From under a fur-trimmed hat with long flaps, a man searched my face.

Startled out of my rambling thoughts, I shook my head. I pointed at the bakery. "Just headed there." My words probably came out more clipped than I had intended. The cold made me miserable. I forced my shoulders down away from my ears and fumbled with my hood until I got it up. My dress coat wasn't nearly warm enough, and in my hurry to get on the road, I hadn't thought to bring my heavier one.

Maybe coming here had been a mistake.

I adjusted the strap of my purse over my shoulder and took a step forward. The welcome wagon didn't seem in a hurry to leave. My spine stiffened. I felt a bit hemmed in between the two parked vehicles. "Can I help you?" I asked, not hiding my annoyance.

A shadow flickered across his face, gone almost as quickly as it came. He lifted an amused brow that disappeared beneath the brim of his ridiculous hat, and instinctively I took a step back. "No, ma'am," he said, slowly. "I thought maybe…" His words trailed off. "Clearly I was mistaken. Have a good day."

Mistaken?

He wandered back over to the ladder positioned under a garland that was draped over the Top Shelf Brewery sign. He dragged the ladder a few feet down and assessed his handiwork. My pulse thudded in my ears. He worked at the brewery. The business that had been a thorn in my sister's side.

"Kinda chilly for outdoor projects," I said as I maneuvered around the ladder. I wondered what he'd think when he saw me heading into the bakery. He'd probably just think I was a customer. No big deal.

Something about his sly smile sent a hum of awareness coursing through my veins. How was he connected to the brewery? My sister and I still weren't sure how ownership had shaken out after Edward Hemsley's sudden passing.

He'd been the son of the original owner, who was still around —mostly retired, like my grandmother.

Edward's widow had never warmed to us, partially blaming my sister, Sammie, for the stress her husband had been under when he tried expanding the brewery, determined to bulldoze our businesses in the process. We'd refused to vacate, standing our ground against whatever grand plans the brewery had had in mind.

"My boss is a taskmaster," he said, snapping me out of my thoughts.

"Your boss?" The knot in my stomach loosened a fraction. "They've got you out here putting up decorations in a snowstorm?"

He placed a gloved finger over his lips. "Shhh. Jobs don't come easy around here."

I followed his gaze to the bakery next door. A little garland and some string lights would do wonders to spruce the place up for the season, maybe even boost business. "Any chance I could hire you to decorate the front of the bakery?" I tugged my coat collar higher. *Goodness, it was freezing.*

His mouth quirked, but his eyes narrowed slightly. "You work at the bakery?" As if the idea genuinely surprised him.

"Sorta." A gust of wind whipped down the street, and I stepped closer to him, seeking shelter of some sort. His attention shifted to the brewery then back to me, studying me in a way that sent an unexpected prickle of self-consciousness down my spine.

I took a deliberate step backward. "If you're looking for a side job," I said, jerking my thumb toward the bakery, "stop in."

He hooked an arm on a rung of the ladder, his grin widening. "Maybe I will."

The way he looked at me was unnerving. There was an ease to his confidence, the kind of effortless self-assurance only a dangerously charming man in a ridiculous hat could pull off. I knew better than to get involved with that kind of guy, even if it was just harmless banter. I mustered a tight smile, spun around, and made my way to the bakery.

If he actually showed up looking for a job, I'd tell him I'd changed my mind.

Consider it momentary brain freeze.

2 /

ted

I watched her slip into the bakery, escaping the blowing snow. Pulling my glove snugly over the cuff of my sleeve, I turned away from the wind and let out a slow breath. That could've gone smoother. The look she gave me before ducking inside wasn't exactly "I'd like to get to know you better."

Still, something about her struck me. The determined tilt of her chin. The way she squared her shoulders like she had more important places to be.

She looked just like Sammie Martin, formerly Sammie Johnson.

Which meant she probably was who I thought she was.

Emily.

I hadn't seen her since that summer when we were kids. A hint of nostalgia curled in my gut. Those long, endless summer days when I thought this place was the center of the universe, when the future was nothing but open roads and possibility.

Before I decided I wanted *out.*

Before life had a funny way of pulling me back in.

An arctic wind rustled the garland I had painstakingly affixed to the trim of the brewery, snapping me back to the present moment. I had that thing secured against hurricane winds. Or at least I thought I did. I picked up the box of decorations and glanced back toward the bakery. I wondered what Emily would say if I wandered over there and introduced myself.

Did she even remember me? No flicker of recognition had sparked in her pretty blue eyes. I wouldn't exactly be welcomed into the bakery for social hour, unless, of course, I was there to spend some money on my daily pastry and coffee. Sammie was a smart businesswoman and wouldn't refuse a paying customer, but she lacked the instinctual warmth of her grandmother, Cookie. I couldn't blame Sammie. Galina, my dad's much-younger widow, had been ruthless in her push to claim the property. The clashes between them were more than exhausting—some said the stress had given my dad a major heart attack. It was why I came back when I had thought this town had nothing left for me.

I dropped the box of decorations inside the door, then folded up the ladder and cut through the narrow side street alongside the brewery, heading for the alley where I'd parked. I had hoped to finish the Christmas decorations before the snow hit, but the beer delivery had arrived a day early, throwing off my plans. Sorting that out had taken longer than expected. Apparently, everyone had been watching the weather and adjusting accordingly.

I secured the ladder to my truck, bracing against the blowing winds, grateful for my dad's old trapper hat. Every time I wore it, I thought of those early mornings in the woods, hunting with him when I was a kid. We talked a big game about tracking a buck, but mostly we spent the time hunkered down in the tree stand in companionable silence, content just being there. Afternoons were spent by the fire in the cabin, eating all sorts of things that weren't good for us.

Having my dad to myself had been some of the best times

of my life. It was the one time he seemed to let me just *be*—no expectations, no lectures. The rest of the time, he pushed hard, the way competitive men do when they're trying to relive their glory days through their kid. His was football. Mine just so happened to be hockey.

A part of me wondered if building a hockey-themed brewery had been his version of an olive branch. Or maybe he'd simply picked a sport where Walleye Point excelled. The locals still talked about the state championships from a decade ago.

I guessed I'd never really know.

Yet it wasn't the hockey theme that got me back here—it was Dad's heart attack a few months before the opening.

A familiar ache of regret haunted me. It shouldn't have taken his illness for me to mend fences. I was only grateful there had been time before his passing for us to reconnect. Somewhat.

A horn sounded out on Main Street, probably someone losing patience with the deteriorating road conditions. Man, it was only the first week of December. It promised to be a long winter.

I double-checked the tie-downs securing the ladder, then I dug into my pocket for the keys to the alley entrance to the brewery. I smiled to myself, noticing the quickly deteriorating tracks leading from where I stood to the back of the bakery. Big Ed, my grandfather, visited Cookie every chance he got. They had been friends long before the brewery and the subsequent family clashes.

Good for them.

I didn't think even my dad could have predicted the success of the brewery, partially propped up by the redevelopment of the Langmore estate into a hotel and conference center. He never got to see the place thrive. Now it was up to his widow and me. Galina clung to grudges, whereas I was trying to make peace with my new reality. It wasn't just about bricks and mortar anymore.

I inserted the key into the back door and twisted it. I slid into the back office of the brewery, and the solid door thudded behind me, closing off the howling wind. I peeled off my hat and coat and stomped the snow from my boots.

"It's getting pretty wicked out there," I said as I stepped into the main dining room and slid behind the bar. A few tables were filled with locals nursing beers and picking at wings before braving the storm. We had expanded the seating area significantly, and we even hosted parties. Business was booming.

I grabbed the box of Christmas decorations from inside the door and stashed them behind the bar.

"I don't think we're going to have much business tonight." Galina wiped down the counter with a white rag, her movements easy, practiced. My dad's widow, only ten years my senior, had been part of my life for a decade and a half, but since she'd married Dad the summer after I graduated high school, we didn't exactly have a stepmom/stepson relationship.

"It's definitely not letting up." I took a sip of water, but my mind wasn't on the weather. Instead, it drifted back to the woman who'd stepped out of that expensive car. That *very* familiar woman. I wondered what she'd been up to all these years. I ran a hand along my jaw, realizing how much time had passed. We had both lived another lifetime since then.

"Cool. Maybe we'll have a snow day tomorrow," Jayden, my fifteen-year-old nephew, said, snapping me out of my thoughts. He slung one arm over the back of his bar stool like he had all the time in the world. My nephew was the main reason I was sticking around. His mother—my sister—had bailed on him, then his grandfather died. The kid had to know some people stuck around.

"Maybe," I said noncommittally. The town was good at clearing roads. School would probably be open.

Jayden glanced toward the street. The frigid air outside frosted the edges of the window. "Our bus slid through the intersection. It might be too dangerous to go outside."

I chuckled. "Won't they have classes over Zoom?"

"Ugh, do you think so?" His excitement dimmed instantly. "That sucks." He tipped his head back with an exaggerated groan, stretching out the last word like it physically pained him.

Galina and I exchanged looks and laughed. In the three months between my dad's heart attack and death, we'd banded together, keeping both him and the brewery afloat. We were in survival mode. Over the last eighteen months, our partnership had solidified, mostly through the business, but also with an understanding built on shared loss and a desire to keep Jayden on the right path.

The muted buzz of the hand dryer sounded from the men's bathroom down the hall. A moment later, Big Ed appeared in his slim-fit jeans and plaid shirt. "Don't think we'll be getting many more customers tonight."

Galina nudged me with the back of her hand. "You two are beginning to sound alike."

"Nothing wrong with that," I said. "Why don't the three of you take my truck home? I'll stay and close up once that last table finishes up." I could walk the few blocks to my childhood home where we all lived. It was our version of *Modern Family*.

"I made soup. Why don't we eat first?" Galina tossed the bar rag aside, then she lowered her voice. "As soon as the last customers leave, I'll lock the door. We can enjoy a nice meal together here in the dining room."

The brewery's menu was simple: wings, pizza, a few sandwiches, and soup. They had an expanded menu for catered events, which were getting very popular.

Big Ed settled onto a stool and grabbed the TV remote, flipping the channel to some home improvement show.

I gave him a look. "Since when do you like HGTV?"

He drummed his work-worn hands on the bar. "Might need to brush up on the current remodeling trends."

Galina arched a brow. "Oh? Do you know someone who's remodeling?"

Sensing our collective curiosity, Big Ed said, "Where's this soup you were talking about?"

Galina threw up her hands and disappeared into the kitchen. Meanwhile, I cashed out the last customers and locked the door behind them.

When I returned to the bar, Big Ed was staring outside. "Saw that fancy car pull in earlier. Wonder how it does in the snow."

Fifty years of running a bar had made my grandfather an expert at small talk. He could make any question sound like casual curiosity rather than nosiness.

And he missed nothing.

Jayden looked up from stuffing his homework back in his backpack. "Are you talking about the really cool metallic-blue BMW?"

"Is that what they call that color?" Big Ed slid off his stool, went around behind the bar, and pulled the lever on the draft beer.

My nephew shrugged. "It's Maddie's aunt."

"Her aunt?" I said, trying to keep my tone casual as I grabbed a stack of napkins from behind the bar and restocked the holder.

Jayden gave a quick nod. "Her Aunt Emily. She's, like, helping out at the bakery."

"Oh yeah, why?" I asked.

"You didn't hear?" Jayden lowered the lid of his laptop, as if this story needed his full attention. "Maddie's mom had a wicked skiing accident. Smashed up her wrist and can barely walk."

"Yowzah, that's rough."

Outside the window, a fresh layer of snow piled up on Emily's BMW. Whatever she did for work, she did well. That BMW wasn't cheap. A question nudged at the back of my mind, but I shoved it away. I had no business wondering if she was married. It had been a while. Who knew what the years had brought her? Maybe I'd be lucky enough to find out.

My mind drifted to those carefree days of summer, riding my bike around from dawn until dusk. The dwindling days of August when the carnival came to town.

"Ski patrol had to bring her down," Jayden said, sitting ramrod straight in his chair. "Her helmet was cracked." He was back to discussing Emily's sister's accident.

"Good thing she had it on," Galina said. Her tone had that pointed edge, the kind adults used to make sure their lessons stuck. Clearly, she wanted to leave an impression on Jayden.

"So, Maddie said her aunt's taking over the bakery for a bit?" I hoped it sounded like small talk, but I had my doubts.

Jayden's voice took on that familiar warmth, the one that surfaced whenever he mentioned Emily's niece. I knew better than to comment on how much he talked about her. It seemed he had a crush. My heart tugged at the memory of my own teenage crush.

Apparently, she drove a fancy BMW, wore fancier clothes, and had no recollection of me.

A smile pulled at my lips.

Maybe it was the hat.

3 /
emily

I stepped into the bakery, pushed back my hood, and paused. The warmth wrapped around me like a hug I didn't know I needed. The scent of sugar, vanilla, and a hint of coffee was so familiar it almost knocked the breath out of me. My stomach rumbled in response.

I slipped out of my coat, already missing its insulation, and glanced down at my hands. No gloves. No hat. Not thorough planning on my part. I'd packed an entire suitcase and somehow forgotten the winter basics.

Across the room, my niece stood behind the dessert case, head down, fingers tapping away on her phone. I cleared my throat, and she glanced up, her initial flash of annoyance—the spitting image of the scowl my sister used to give me daily—vanishing in an instant.

Pure joy took its place.

She scooted around the counter and threw her arms around me. "Aunt Emily! You made it," she said quietly into my shoulder.

"Did you have any doubt?" I smoothed a hand over her silky hair, a shade lighter than my own. I pulled back from our embrace and studied her face, feeling a warm affection that my day-to-day life was otherwise devoid of. "Hey, you got your braces off."

Maddie flashed me an exaggerated grin, revealing perfectly straight teeth.

"Very nice."

"Thank goodness. I was the last of my friends with a full mouth of metal." She held up a finger before hurrying back behind the counter. "I have to box up a pickup order. Give me a second."

The bakery was empty except for the two of us. Not much had changed since my summers in Walleye Point. Sun-bleached photos of sailboats, the lighthouses of the Great Lakes, and my sister and me with Cookie at various ages lined the walls.

"Someone must really need a sugar fix to come out in this weather," I said.

Maddie lifted a shoulder as she folded the box flaps. "I don't ask questions."

"Are you old enough to be working here alone?" I glanced around, half-expecting to see my sister emerge from the back.

"I'm sixteen. Lucky for Mom because she has me filling in all the time." Her voice carried a touch of weariness, like this wasn't just an after-school job but an actual obligation. I had a feeling those paychecks weren't only going toward trendy crop tops.

"I thought she hired someone to work afternoons," I said.

Maddie set the order on the top of the dessert case and came around and flopped down at one of the new tables. My sister had been determined to turn the bakery into a bakery/coffee shop. "She quit."

I might have missed the flush of red on her cheeks if I hadn't been watching her. What was that all about?

"Now it's just me and Mom working here. And Cookie when she's not doing other stuff. And now that Mom crashed into a tree..." The last comment held none of the sympathy it warranted.

My grandmother had sold the business to her granddaughters so she could retire, something she didn't seem to relish, except for when she was managing the remodel of her new place. She'd found a charming little cottage that needed more love than she'd admit, but it was within walking distance of town, and that, apparently, was the real selling point.

"Is your great-grandmother here?" I tilted my head toward the back room. What I would do to see Cookie emerge with a sweet treat. My stomach grumbled again. I really needed something balanced to eat.

"She went home." Maddie stretched out and crossed her legs at the ankles. "Wanted to beat the storm."

My eyes widened. "Does she still drive?"

"Sometimes," Maddie said, as if she hadn't given it much thought. "How far away did you have to park?"

"Not far. I caught someone pulling out."

Maddie pressed her lips together. "Mom's been complaining that she's losing customers because there's nowhere to park."

"The brewery next door?" I asked. My sister would probably find any reason to be annoyed with them. I couldn't blame her. The town board seemed to be overly involved in our business during the brewery's construction, as if they wanted to give us a reason to sell.

"Yep." Maddie shrugged. "And now that Mom's out of commission..." She shook her head then grabbed one side of her University at Buffalo hoodie and pulled it off, revealing her cropped top.

Wait. Is that a belly button piercing?

She caught me staring and shot me a look, one that made her seem years older, before leaning in and whispering conspiratorially, "It's a poop show around here."

A smile tugged at the corners of my lips. I appreciated her effort to censor herself. Not that I cared if she cursed, but I could already hear my sister blaming me for corrupting her child.

"It is *not* a poop show."

I spun toward the voice. Sammie emerged from the back room on one of those scooter things, one leg propped up. She maneuvered carefully, her hand and casted wrist poking out of a blue sling.

"You should be home resting," I said, rushing to greet her. I shifted my focus to Maddie. "Why didn't you tell me your mom was here?"

Maddie shrugged, not moving from her slouched position.

"And you're supposed to be in Pittsburgh," my sister said. "I told you I had everything under control." She narrowed her gaze at Maddie. "This was *your* doing, right?"

She shrugged again, and I wasn't about to rat her out. My niece's first text came right after she found out her mom was in a skiing accident, and they continued, shifting from concern to annoyance that there was no one to help at the bakery. My style wasn't to throw someone under the bus, even though I had texted back and forth with Maddie informing her of my plans over the past twenty-four hours. I had hoped that she might have told her mom.

Yeah, I could have called, but I knew Sammie would never admit she needed help. Our mother had raised us both to be strong and independent. So I had made an executive decision to show up without telling my sister and deal with the fallout later.

"You should have told me you were coming," Sammie said.

"Then you would have told me you had everything under control."

She rested her good arm on the handle of the scooter. "I do have everything under control." Her clipped comment gave no room for interpretation, and I was careful to keep my expression neutral so as not to offend her.

"You didn't need to pull your aunt away from work." Sammie gave her daughter a pointed glare. "We both know how busy she is."

The jab landed low and familiar. She wasn't wrong. I didn't make it to Walleye Point as often as I should, and I usually let my bank account do the heavy lifting when it came to being the helpful sister. But still, I thought they'd cut me some slack. I did what I could.

I swallowed a zinger that would have only added fuel to the fire. Sammie had always had a knack for pushing my buttons. Instead, I pasted on a smile that I hoped didn't look as fake as it felt.

"Lucky for you, I've got some free time. And I'm here." Even I didn't buy my cheery tone. It wasn't exactly me.

With an exaggerated roll of her eyes, my sister said, "Free time? Since when? Last year you skipped Christmas because you were too busy."

Last year I had been in the middle of a big merger. My company was buying a sub shop chain, and I had to make sure all the financials were in order. "Let's just say I'm between jobs." I had carved out a career that afforded me the luxury of being picky. Of leaving a job when I wanted and of carefully choosing my next opportunity. I had a financial cushion and a skill set that made me employable, not that I'd rub that in my sister's face, especially when she was down on her luck. And that was the kind of thinking that would make me sound like a complete jerk, so I kept it to myself.

Growing up, it had always been me and Sammie against the world. My mom had fostered that too. She had lost her only sister in a car accident when they were teenagers, and she encouraged us to look out for one another.

You never know what's around the corner.

As a result, Sammie—only older by eighteen months—

and I had done everything together. She was the outgoing sister; I was the shy, quiet one. But she never made me feel like the odd one out. And I loved her for that.

This would be Sammie's first holiday season without Cookie at the helm of the bakery. Breaking a few bones probably hadn't been on my sister's bingo card.

I cleared my throat and chose my words carefully. "I can stay and help run the bakery. Honestly, it's no problem."

"I can hire someone. Really, it's no problem," Sammie said, parroting my words back to me with enough edge to make her point.

"Mom, come on," Maddie said. "No one wants to work here."

Sammie's brows jumped, but she quickly smoothed her expression. "The last hire didn't pan out, but..." Her jaw twitched, and for a second, I thought she might actually say what she was thinking. Instead, she let her eyes linger on the nearly empty dessert case. "We'll find someone."

She clicked the scooter brake then maneuvered herself into the chair beside it. She looked like she was running on fumes.

"Listen, I know it's hard to get holiday help. Let me do this." A pulse ticked in my head. Why was my sister so reluctant to accept my offer? I genuinely wanted to help her power through this holiday season, and not just because I had a financial investment in this place. I wanted to make sure this business flourished so that my sister didn't have to struggle like our mother had when we were growing up. Our mother had drilled the lesson of financial independence into us too.

When the silence stretched a beat too long, Maddie reached over and touched her mom's arm. "Basketball season started. I don't want to miss any more games."

I tilted my head, genuinely impressed. "You play?"

That earned me matching laughs with the same tilt of the

head and crinkle at the corners of their eyes. Everything about them marked them as mother and daughter.

"No," Maddie said, pressing a hand to her chest like I'd wounded her. "I made varsity cheerleading."

"Oooh, excuse me," I said, dragging it out, complete with an exaggerated eye roll. "Congrats on making varsity cheer."

My mind went to the exchange I'd witnessed out front. Perhaps that boy Maddie had been talking to played basketball? How quaint, my niece the cheerleader and "her friend" the basketball player. There was probably a Taylor Swift lyric in there, and a lot of assumptions on my part too. Since I didn't want to alienate my niece, I kept my thoughts to myself. Maybe Sammie didn't realize she was talking to a boy. Wouldn't surprise me. She'd been a pro at hiding things from Mom and Grandma when we were kids. And it wasn't like I was any more transparent. I just didn't have much worth hiding.

"So how about it? I can help you through the holiday season," I said with that forced cheer again, as I suddenly got an urge to check my emails. "Maddie gets to cheer. Everyone lives happily ever after."

My sister looked up from her attempts at reaching an itch under her wrist cast with a straw. "Cookie doesn't mind helping." If Sammie had meant to sound convincing, she had gone for the wrong tone. According to Maddie, her great-grandmother was thoroughly enjoying her retirement, coming and going as she pleased. Keeping a schedule wasn't on *her* bingo card.

"We can go round and round," I said flatly. "Or you can agree to let me help."

"Where are you going to stay?" Sammie asked in a tone that didn't exactly sound like a personal invitation.

"I thought maybe…"

"Cookie is staying in my extra bedroom until her new place is ready. I don't have space."

"Oh." I swiped a hand across my mouth, more to buy time than anything. I hadn't expected a warm welcome, but I didn't realize how hard she'd push back once I showed up anyway. I wasn't exactly thrilled about staying in a hotel. The Langmore's rates felt a little excessive for a month-long stay, and word on the street was that the old inn could host a Bates Motel reboot.

"How about the apartment upstairs?" Maddie said.

"What happened to Norm?" My heart dropped. For as long as I could remember, a friendly old man had rented the apartment above Cookie's bakery. Thinking back, he had always been old. Our grandmother would have us run up there with baked goods on occasion. He'd tip us a dollar. "Did he..." I was surprised by the emotion clogging my throat.

"He moved in with his daughter in Buffalo," Sammie said, seemingly unfazed by my sudden wave of nostalgia. I didn't make it back to Walleye Point often, but some part of me liked to believe nothing here would change.

"How long has the apartment been empty?" I worked to smooth the crease between my brows, not wanting to come off as judgmental. I had a financial investment in the bakery but a hands-off approach. I had bought the building so Cookie could retire and paid for the kitchen remodel after a few suspiciously timed complaints from the health department. I'd promised I wouldn't interfere in the business. The deal was simple: five years to grow the business, then we'd discuss repayment terms. I saw it as an investment in both the bakery and my sister's independence. And judging by how often she vented about her lazy husband, I figured she'd need something she could count on.

"His daughter helped him move out in April," Sammie said.

I tried to remember what I'd had going on in April. Oh, right, that was when I got slammed with the New York project. Lots of travel, nonstop meetings. No wonder their tenant moving out never came up. I'd probably kept our calls short that month, though Sammie and I always stayed in touch. Sort of.

"I listed it as an Airbnb," Sammie said. "I made more in the summer months than I had renting it all year."

I tucked in my chin. "Go you."

"You're not the only one with business savvy." My sister smiled brightly, clearly pleased with herself.

"Yes!" Maddie pumped her fist. "Aunt Emily can stay in the Airbnb, and I won't miss cheer practice."

I looked to Sammie, forcing myself not to steamroll ahead like I always did. "That okay with you?"

She sighed. "I'm still the boss. Even now." She gestured from head to toe, her cast and sling making the statement even more dramatic.

"You're the boss," I said.

I figured I could do anything for one month.

4 /
emily

I slipped the key into the lock and wiggled the glass doorknob. It took a little coaxing before the mechanism gave a reluctant click. I released a small breath of victory and pushed open the door to the Airbnb over the bakery. *Phew.* I'd had serious doubts that Sammie had grabbed the right key from the junk drawer under the register, considering how she'd squinted at it, her nose scrunched up like the past renters had done something to it.

I dragged my luggage in from the landing. As a kid, I had only been this far while delivering a donut to Norm, who seemed ancient even then. I was glad he had been able to live as long as he had independently.

Once inside the apartment, I dropped my purse on a floral-upholstered chair that sat under a window. Light from a lamppost cut across the hardwood floor and up the opposite wall. The view of Main Street below was picturesque. The steadily falling snow blanketed the sleepy town, making me feel like I was completely alone.

I drew closer to the window. The glass felt cool against my cheek. Below, a misshapen mound of snow was the only sign my car was even there. There had to be at least two feet out there. Shuddering, I drew the blinds and switched on a lamp.

Warm light bathed the cozy room, chasing away the chill. A smile tugged at my lips.

If Sammie had been the one to decorate this small space, she had done a great job. I was especially drawn to the over-sized furniture, side table, and small bookshelf filled with popular paperbacks. A perfect reading nook under the window.

With a cursory glance at the cute kitchenette with cow accents—Sammie loved cows—I dragged my suitcase into the small room tucked under a dormer. The inviting shades of blue and the Scottish Highland cow design on the decorative pillows should have put me at ease, but instead the familiar weight of concern pressed down on my chest.

Why hadn't Sammie mentioned the Airbnb? It was a great idea. If she could keep it rented, it might offset any bakery losses. I exhaled slowly. I figured I should go through the financials while I was in town. I had promised to be a silent partner, but surely Sammie wouldn't object to a little profes-sional expertise.

I'd have to tread lightly.

Before hopping in the shower, I did a quick email check for any updates from Blue Moon. Still nothing. No formal offer, no extra pre-offer hoops to jump through. I always managed to land on my feet, but that didn't mean companies made the process painless. Interviews, follow-ups, and onboarding were like a corporate obstacle course no one knew how to train for.

The hot shower helped unknot my shoulders, at least temporarily. Afterward, I checked my phone again. Then my email. The waiting was officially getting old. And there wasn't a darn thing I could do about it.

The stillness pressed in around me, making my skin itch. I was used to the hum of city traffic outside my apartment at all hours. Could I even fall asleep in this kind of quiet? And if I did, I had a feeling I'd be up at dawn.

I set my phone face down on the nightstand to reduce screen time, but it didn't last long. I scooped it up and did my usual scrolling, adding weather to the cycle of news, email, and Instagram.

Well, I must have drifted off to sleep because I found myself in a pool of sweat with my phone pressed under my cheek. I tossed back the covers and flopped my legs on top of them in exasperation. After getting my bearings, I sat up. A bead of sweat rolled down my back. A soft light outlined the thin shade on the window. It had to be close to dawn.

Under the window, the radiator hissed.

Ugh. The culprit for this unbearable sweat box.

When I adjusted the knob, it broke off in my hand. *Just great.* I examined the knob and tried unsuccessfully to thread it back on its stem. The stifling heat and my frustration compounded the headache forming behind my eyes.

I straightened and opened the blinds. The first hint of purple colored the horizon, signaling the calm after the storm. White blanketed the entire town, creating a clean slate for the day ahead. I'd need my coffee while I waited for the rest of the world to wake up.

I grabbed my laptop and the crocheted blanket that had been draped over the chair by the window then headed downstairs to the bakery. Thankfully, a second stairway led to the kitchen in the back of the bakery, sparing me from having to use the one that led directly outside while still in my PJs. Reaching the bakery, I checked the thermostat. Seventy degrees. Comfortable enough.

Thank goodness.

Using only the soft light pouring in from the large front window, I figured out how to operate the coffee maker thanks to the laminated, detailed instructions next to it. Last night, Sammie had made the decision to delay the opening of the store until ten a.m., giving the plows time to clear the snow from the streets.

The coffee maker hissed and brewed up a wonderfully fragrant cup of coffee. I had finished mixing in creamer I'd found in the short fridge under the counter when a day-old donut caught my eye. I paused, mentally wrestling with myself.

Don't do it.

Yes, do it. When was the last time you ate a cream-filled powdered donut?

Just thinking about it made my stomach growl. Not wanting to delay my sister and niece getting home in the storm last night, I had told them I'd had a huge lunch and wasn't hungry. It seemed like a harmless fib until I woke up ravenous.

Desperate times called for desperate measures. I slid open the glass bakery case, and the sweet smell of the few remaining baked goods made my mouth water. I snagged the donut, straightened, and took a bite. I closed my eyes and lost myself in the sugary explosion. If a snowstorm wasn't the perfect time to indulge, I didn't know when was.

I took my coffee, donut, and a stack of mail I'd found tucked between a mug of pens and a tape dispenser over to one of the tables along the wall where I had set down my laptop, careful to place my back to the window. I rolled my shoulders. Once I'd stopped sweating, my skin felt cool. I wrapped the blanket around my shoulders and opened my email, setting the envelopes aside.

Checking on my life in Pittsburgh while back here felt as incongruous as my big sister taking over this business from my grandmother. Once upon a time, we *both* had bigger dreams than Walleye Point. What had once been summers of fun with our grandmother had turned into us begging our mom to let us hang by the town pool with our friends back home by the time we reached high school.

Our mom was having none of it.

I finally broke the routine at sixteen. Or technically it was

Sammie who shattered it when she announced she was pregnant weeks after high school graduation. The dad was Trevor, a decent-enough townie with a steady job and no real plans. Turns out, spending summers in Walleye Point didn't make us immune to standard-issue teenage drama.

The next summer, between my junior and senior years, I stayed in Buffalo with my regular friends while Sammie remained permanently in Walleye Point, locking in her future with a baby and a backyard wedding.

The following fall, I went off to college. Alone. It had been *our* dream. Sammie would go first, and I'd follow. We'd graduate, land dream jobs, and share a shoebox apartment in New York City, à la *Felicity* or *Sex and the City*.

But that last summer in Walleye Point had changed everything. Suddenly, it was on me to fulfill Mom's vision of getting the degree, landing the big job, and staying financially independent, no matter what.

Still, sometimes I wondered if Sammie had wound up with the better deal. She grumbled about Trevor sometimes, but she had Maddie. That kid was amazing. Maybe the chaos had come with its own kind of reward.

I dragged a finger across the trackpad of my laptop, trying to shut out the chorus of overthinking in my head and focus on my inbox. Then I saw it.

Subject: *We'd love to have you on the team.*

My heart did a little backflip. I clicked the email, holding my breath as my eyes raced across the message. *We're finalizing some internal logistics and hope to move forward quickly. In the meantime, we wanted to let you know how excited we are about the possibility of having you join the team.*

Oh my. Oh my. My mouth went dry.

We'll be in touch very soon with more details.

So, still no actual offer? Icy dread settled in my stomach. Had I jumped the gun by quitting my job? No. No, I knew my worth. The hiring manager said I was a shoo-in. These things just took time.

I squared my shoulders, fired off a breezy thank-you email expressing my gratitude for their continued interest and saying that I was looking forward to the next steps, and closed my laptop with purpose. I wasn't going to let this half answer ruin my day.

Blue Moon was crossing their *t*'s and dotting their *i*'s. That was all.

The morning light filtering in from outside was enough to see by to go through the junk mail that had come into the bakery. It was mostly credit card offers and coupons. I was about to call it a bust when I found unopened mail addressed simply to Current Resident at 599 Main Street. I scanned the flyer. Apparently, the town was encouraging all the businesses to decorate for the holidays, and the winner would receive free advertising on a billboard on the Thruway. The town seemed to want to take advantage of the brand-new hotel and conference center, a brewery, and whatever other businesses were popping up to increase tourism.

I turned the flyer over, trying to figure out when it had been sent. The postmark was illegible. That was probably why the brewery next door was pulling out all the stops with the storefront decorations. My competitive nature got my brain spinning, imagining what we could do here at the bakery. Sure, why not join in on the holiday spirit? And free advertising couldn't hurt. Gosh, it could really help.

I immediately opened a new tab on my laptop and started shopping for decorations, fully prepared to drop more than a few bucks.

Scrape. Scrape. Scape.

The rhythmic dragging of a shovel against pavement yanked me away from the riveting reviews on an indoor/outdoor automatic timer. I glanced over my shoulder at the large window overlooking Main Street. Someone was already out there, shoveling sidewalks before the town cleared the streets. I checked the time, wondering if it was too early to text Sammie. Had she hired someone for snow removal? Ah, what did it matter? Some winter warrior was shoveling the walks at the crack of dawn. I might as well let them.

I returned my focus to the laptop, but then a rat-tat-tat sounded on the window. I froze then lifted my head and stared straight ahead, wondering if I didn't turn, maybe they wouldn't be able to see me. Or maybe if I was fast enough, I could bolt into the back. Run upstairs.

Rat-tat-tat.

I glanced down at my ratty sleep T-shirt and my PJ shorts. I only had the crocheted blanket to hide under.

If only I could melt into the tile floor and disappear.

Squaring my shoulders, I pulled the blanket tighter around them and glanced behind me. The man with the goofy hat from yesterday was peering into the bakery, using his hand as a visor to see more clearly.

My heart plummeted.

He mimed something with his shovel. Did he want to discuss payment for clearing the walk? Who did Cookie or my sister usually hire? I went to the door, twisting the lock with a little more force than necessary, annoyance battling it out with my complete embarrassment.

Careful to keep the blanket tight around my shoulders, I pulled open the door. An arctic blast hit the exposed skin of my legs and face. I tucked one leg in front of the other and did my best to hide behind the door. Fat lot of good that did. It was made of glass.

"Morning," he said, too cheery for this early. "I got the sidewalks cleared. Crews should be out soon to plow the roads."

"Thanks." I should have said more, but I wasn't exactly in a chatty mood.

He pressed his lips together. "I take it you stayed in the Airbnb."

I dragged my lower lip through my teeth. If I hadn't met this man briefly yesterday and known that he was employed by the brewery, I might have felt a little creeped out that he knew so much about me. But this was a small town. Where everyone knew everything. Only one of the many reasons I couldn't believe my big sister had hitched her wagon to a man she had met while visiting our grandmother. It was almost like wrapping an anchor around your ankle and jumping into the deep end.

You're being judgy…

I sighed. "Yes, I'm Sammie's sister. I'm here to help with the bakery while she recovers from her skiing accident." I mentioned it like he'd know what I was talking about because I was sure he would. Small town and all.

"Hello, Sammie's sister." There was something familiar about the twinkle in his eyes, like a half-remembered joke I wasn't quite in on.

I felt a smile threaten and promptly strangled it. "Emily."

"Ted." He nodded once, easy and confident like he wasn't standing there in the freezing cold, wearing that ridiculous hat.

"Nice to meet you," I said, tightening the blanket around my shoulders like it could shield me from more than just the weather. "Do you need anything else?"

My eyes drifted to the snow-covered lump formerly known as my car. Not exactly the morning workout I had in mind.

Ted followed my gaze. "I can dig it out for you."

Of course he could. Why wouldn't the guy from the rival business offer to rescue me before I even got dressed?

"I can't ask you to do that," I said quickly. "It's fine." Unless he accepted Venmo. Or an invoice. I wasn't about to owe favors to someone affiliated with the brewery that had been circling our family bakery, waiting for us to go out of business.

His grin was slow and maddeningly charming. "Why can't you ask me?"

I hesitated. That was the problem. I didn't have a good answer.

And maybe that was what made me the tiniest bit nervous.

ted

I did my best not to stare.

Emily clutched the blanket at her neck, gripping the fabric like a lifeline. Still, she shivered. Not surprising, considering her bare legs peeked out from beneath the colorful crocheted throw.

I could have suggested she go inside, but I wasn't ready to say goodbye. Inviting myself in would raise questions, so instead I stood there bundled up in full winter gear, talking to a girl I once knew who was still in her PJs.

She'd probably wandered downstairs for coffee, expecting a quiet morning of work, not some guy knocking on the window this early. Her messy bun, flawless skin, and makeup-free face were a stark contrast to the version of Emily I'd run into yesterday. That Emily had strutted into town in high-heeled boots designed more for fashion than function, a perfectly made-up face, and a car that cost more than most homes around here.

Not exactly the sixteen-year-old Emily I remembered.

Nor was she the type of woman I usually went for.

And yet, the second she had stepped out of her car into the snowstorm, something about her had pulled me in. I wasn't able to put my finger on it until I realized who she was. Then it made perfect sense.

Not that I'd act on it. Though it sure would be fun to try.

"Well, I'm going to clear off your car whether you ask me to or not." I ran a hand across my jaw. "Just promise you won't try to drive on the roads until the plows go through."

"Okay," she said, somewhat resigned.

"Are you working?" I asked, half to keep the conversation going, half because I felt like a heel for interrupting her morning.

It was a happy coincidence finding her up this early. Did she really not know who I was? Not that it was surprising. Back when she spent summers here, I was just the grandson of the guy who ran the hole-in-the-wall bar next door. Teens didn't exactly keep tabs on local business legacies.

Wondering what someone did for a living was more of an adult pastime.

I only knew her as Emily back then. The girl who sort of broke my heart when we were both sixteen. I say sort of because, really, what did a couple of teenagers know about love? But still, it stung.

I was just grabbing a couple of donuts at the bakery when I saw her face—my Emily—smiling back at me from one of the photos Cookie had hung on the wall. I froze, a wave of awkward teenage memories crashing over me. The ones I'd tucked away, telling myself it didn't matter, that it hadn't been that serious.

I'd never breathed a word of our summer fling to anyone. I had my pride. But every once in a while, I'd catch myself wondering what happened to Emily Johnson, surprised that our paths had never crossed again.

Until yesterday.

"Just surfing the web," she said.

I had to claw my way back to the present moment to

remember that I had asked her if she had been working. "Well, sorry to interrupt all the same."

She waved her hand vaguely. Maybe her coolness had less to do with me personally and more to do with my connection to the brewery. No doubt she'd either heard about or been directly involved with the battles between our businesses back when my father was pushing for expansion. I hadn't been involved then, at least not until his heart attack forced me to step in.

I'd learned fast how things worked in small-town politics. My dad had plenty of friends in Walleye Point, and he hadn't thought twice about using those connections to grease the wheels and get what he wanted.

What he hadn't expected was for the bakery to put up such a fight.

Fighting dirty in business wasn't my style. But Emily didn't know that.

I had to walk a fine line—honoring my father's memory by making sure the brewery was a success while proving to the neighbors that I wasn't here to strong-arm anyone. Galina and I had been running Top Shelf for almost two years. Hopefully, any conflict between the businesses was behind us.

Except for parking. And tearing down the bakery for a small parking garage would ease that burden. However, any attempt to buy the bakery had been met with resistance. So, maybe it *wasn't* all behind us.

"I'll let you get back to it," I said, feeling like a heel for making her freeze in the doorway.

"Come in a second," she said, surprising me. I followed her inside, and the door closed hard behind us, as if saying good riddance to the cold. "Can you twist the lock on that? I don't want anyone to come by thinking we're open for business."

"Sure thing."

Humor touched her beautiful blue eyes. "Present

company excluded. I do appreciate that you cleared the snow." The crocheted blanket slipped off one shoulder, revealing bare skin and the thin strap of her PJs. She smiled sheepishly and adjusted the colorful blanket up around her shoulders. "Let me get you some coffee as a thanks." She jerked her thumb toward the refrigerated glass case that usually held a full array of fantastic baked goods. Obviously, the storm had impacted the usual deliveries, and neither Cookie nor Sammie could make it in to bake.

"If it's not too much trouble," I said.

"Not at all."

"Does my sister have a contract with you?" She shifted from foot to foot, and her toes were painted pink.

One of my eyebrows drew down, and I was momentarily confused. "A contract?" A smile tugged at the corner of my lips. *That's right.* I'm the handyman from next door. "Nope. Just being a friendly neighbor."

"Have a seat." She tipped her head toward a table then slipped behind the counter. "I figured out this fancy coffee machine once. Second time should be a breeze."

I pulled off my hat, and my scalp was starting to tingle. The hissing and spurting of the coffee machine were the only sounds in the dimly lit bakery. "I didn't mean to keep you standing in the cold. You must be frozen like a popsicle stick."

"It's okay," she muttered then grunted as she inspected something on the shiny silver machine.

"Need help?" I asked, propping one elbow on the table. My expertise maxed out at operating a Keurig or Mr. Coffee, but I figured it was polite to offer.

"Nope." She flipped a few more levers then spun around, a triumphant smile on her face. "I got it." A pink that wasn't there before touched her cheeks.

I shrugged off my heavy coat, draping it over the back of a chair, then checked my cell phone mindlessly. A short time later, she returned with two steaming mugs then darted back to grab cream and sugar before settling into the seat across from me.

"Thank you," I said, tearing open a sugar packet.

She leaned forward slightly, her eyes sharp. "Do you know my sister?" She said it in the way people do when they already know the answer.

I grinned. "Sure. I'm in here most mornings. I enjoy a cinnamon bun as much as the next guy." I playfully pointed at her. "But I'll tell you what I miss… those apple turnovers Cookie used to make. Remember those? Best apple turnovers I've ever had."

My comment seemed to take Emily off guard, her expression growing soft. "I do remember those. I wonder why she doesn't make them anymore."

"You'll have to ask her." I laughed.

"Cookie is retired," she said.

"Seems to be in a lot for someone who is retired." I watched her take a sip while holding the blanket closed at her neck.

"Doesn't surprise me, but either way, they're going to need help." She fidgeted in her seat, clearing her throat. "You heard about Sammie's accident?"

"I did. How's she doing?" I asked, keeping my tone light.

"Impatient. She wants to get back to work, but her injuries make it all but impossible."

"That's gotta be tough. I take it you're here to help in the meantime?"

She nodded then lifted the mug to her lips.

"How long do you plan on staying?" I picked up the cream and poured a healthy dose into my mug.

"Through the holidays."

"Ah…" I tried to act casual. "What do you do when you're not rescuing your sister's bakery?"

"Finance. Nothing exciting." She stared unseeing over her mug toward the street.

"Where do you live?" I dragged a hand through my hair, realizing it was probably a mess from my hat.

"Pittsburgh. But I grew up in Buffalo and spent a lot of summers here with my grandmother, so I'm not exactly new to town." She paused, her gaze settling on mine, suddenly sharper, like she was seeing me in a different light. "Did you grow up here?"

"I did." I debated telling her that we had met, but before I had a chance, she reached over and pulled out a flyer that had been tucked under a corner of her laptop. She opened it and showed it to me. Ah, the holiday lights competition.

"Any chance I could hire you to put up decorations? I'll make it worth your time," she said when I didn't answer immediately. Her cheeks grew a deeper shade of red, as if she had realized she might have left something up to interpretation. "I mean, money. I can pay you well. I don't want it to affect your job at the brewery, but I'm not a fan of getting on a ladder." The words seemed to tumble out of her. There was something vulnerable about her sitting across from me in her PJs with a blanket wrapped around her shoulders. I had to put her out of her misery.

"Of course. I'd be happy to help out." I studied her over the top of my coffee mug. "Does Cookie have Christmas decorations in back?"

"I'll check, but I'm"—she tapped the lid of her closed laptop— "ordering a few things. They should be here tomorrow. Unless, well, the weather." She worried her bottom lip. "Will it be okay if you do the job for us? Your boss might not like it if we win the competition." A light sparked in her eyes, reminding me of the sense of humor I had been drawn to that day at the carnival.

"Why do you think yours will be better?" I asked playfully.

"I do have exquisite taste."

"We'll see." I held up my mug in a quasi-toast. "It all comes down to execution."

"Are you saying you won't give it your all when hanging my decorations?"

"I always give it my all." I enjoyed seeing the pink rise in her cheeks.

Outside, a snowplow barreled down the street, sending heavy wet snow splatting against the window and making us jump.

Emily drew in a deep breath and released it. "It's going to be a long day."

Maybe. But it had suddenly gotten a lot more interesting.

Emily's phone dinged on the table next to her. She glanced at it then looked back up. "It's Cookie checking in. I should probably give her a call. See how I can be of use while I'm stuck here." She pushed slightly back from the table. That was my cue to go, so I stood.

"Hey, how did you make it in with the weather?" she asked.

"I have a big truck, and I don't live far."

She gave me a quick nod.

I snagged a pen from the table, scratched my cell phone number on a napkin, and patted it with my hand. "Text me when the decorations arrive, and I'll help you out as soon as I have room in my schedule."

"That would be great."

I smiled to myself at the irony. Emily Johnson was back in town, and she had no idea who I was.

Maybe I could make a better second impression.

6 /
emily

After the handyman from the brewery left, I relocked the door and hustled through the back room and up the stairs to the apartment. No way was I risking another small-town do-gooder popping in while I was still in my jammies.

A flush of embarrassment crept up my neck when I caught my reflection in the bathroom mirror. No makeup, serious bedhead, and sleep creases etched across one cheek. Stunning.

What on earth had gotten into me? Inviting him in like we were long-lost brunch buddies, chatting away like I didn't look like I'd just crawled out of a laundry pile.

Apparently, extended solo time had short-circuited my social judgment. And really, it wasn't about him. It was about efficiency. Getting those decorations up required manpower, and he was conveniently available. I was being practical. Laser-focused. Task-oriented.

That was my story, anyway.

I yanked out the elastic in my hair and ran my fingers through it. Why did I care what I looked like? It wasn't like I was going to get involved with the guy who did odd jobs around the brewery. It didn't matter how hot he was when he yanked off that big fuzzy hat. His light-brown eyes had seemed to search mine, giving me his full attention. I was used to having to fight for it in my job. Sure, I demanded it, but it was nice to receive it freely.

A shudder coursed through me, this time having nothing to do with the chill in the air. Shaking my head, I drew back the shower curtain and turned on the water.

After I climbed out and wrapped my hair in the towel, I sighed and pressed the tender flesh under my eyes. I had been working day and night in finance for the past eight years and thought this change of pace for a few weeks would be good. But already I had dealt with a snowstorm and the ever-so-helpful, *hot* handyman from next door. Not that the latter was much of a problem. Unless I made it one.

Ted, that was his name.

I tugged off my towel and ran a comb through my hair. As much as a holiday fling sounded appealing, it wasn't a smart idea. I was leaving right after the holidays.

Get a grip, Emily. He's a nice guy who has offered to help during a snowstorm. That's what people do in a small town. That's it.

My cell phone buzzed right off the edge of the sink and landed with a hard clatter on the tile floor, startling me. I snagged it, relieved the screen hadn't shattered. *Mom.*

I forced a smile and swiped to answer. "Hi, Mom."

"I can't believe you drove in that snowstorm," she said, as if she weren't sitting just east of here under the same gloomy skies in Buffalo.

"Did your granddaughter tell you I was here?" I asked.

"No, Sammie called last night. That girl takes too many risks."

"Nothing that time won't heal. And I can help run this place through the holidays," I said, rummaging through my suitcase for my hair dryer.

"I'm surprised you have time." Her tone was light, but

there was an edge to it. Like she would've preferred I didn't because if *I* had time, that meant she didn't have an excuse not to drop everything and help.

"It's fine, Mom. My new job doesn't start until January." Mostly true. Unless the latest vague email from Blue Moon Investment Group was corporate speak for "we're about to ghost you."

"I want to make sure Sammie makes it through her first holiday season." I tossed the phone on the bed and got dressed.

"She should have let Ed Hemsley buy the property when she had a chance," Mom said, as if it were as simple as that.

I sat down on the edge of the bed. We'd been over this already. Ad nauseam.

If Cookie and Sammie had sold the property to the brewery, they would have barely broken even after paying back taxes and the mortgage. "Sammie is excited about making the bakery her own. She has big plans for a coffee shop." I wasn't sure why I kept repeating this. It never seemed to move the needle with Mom.

Before I got involved, Sammie had planned to pay Cookie a monthly stipend to supplement her Social Security. Then I offered another proposition. I'd buy the property and pay the back taxes, giving Cookie a more secure retirement and freeing Sammie to grow the business without being buried under past debts. We'd figure out repayment down the road.

It should have been considered a win-win, except Mom didn't see it that way.

"Are you going to continue to sink money into that place?" The accusation in her tone grated on my nerves. I loved my mother dearly, but her regrets had made her hard on her daughters. She wanted more for us.

"If I have to," I said. But I had faith in Sammie. She had a plan to grow the business by expanding it into a coffee shop. It might just work. I never thought Walleye Point could support a new hotel and conference center *and* a brewery. But they all seemed to be thriving. Just as importantly, I didn't want my sister—who had married at eighteen and had Maddie at nineteen—to be totally dependent on her seemingly unreliable husband, Trevor. I made more money than I needed, and if this was the only way Sammie would take it, so be it. I found myself smiling. My co-workers bought vacation homes, boats, and other toys while I did something more satisfying.

My mother sighed over the line. "You have a good heart, sweetie. But maybe it would be better if your sister found her footing in a more stable business. That place has been a money pit."

"Let's give it some time."

My mother started to say something else, but my grandmother's name popped up on the screen. "Mom, I need to get this call."

"Oh, okay. Stay warm."

"You too. Love you."

"Love you too."

I switched over. "Morning, Cookie. I saw your text from earlier. I was going to call, but Mom got me first."

"Oh, how is she? Probably had plenty to say about Sammie's accident," Cookie said. They both had my mother pegged.

"Yeah, something like that."

"Anyway," Cookie said, clearly wanting to move on, "how do the roads look out your way?"

"The plows have been down Main Street, but I hear there's more snow coming. I don't think it'll be worth it to open the bakery."

"Yes, the deliveries won't make it in." I could imagine Cookie standing in my sister's kitchen, tapping the eraser end of a pencil on a pad of paper. She had been a list maker for as long as I could remember.

"What can I do since I'll be stuck here all day?" I had been impressed by the commercial kitchen installed after the first slate of complaints from the health department. *Ugh, no wonder Sammie was so annoyed by the brewery.* It seemed too coincidental that the complaints started shortly after Sammie refused the first offer to sell to the Hemsleys. "Maybe I could bake," I said, partially joking but also realizing I'd go stir crazy if I hung out here without anything to do besides check email.

"Do you remember how?" Cookie asked with a lightness in her tone that was lacking in my mother's earlier call.

"I learned from the best." I grabbed a sweatshirt out of my suitcase, set the phone down, and pulled it over my head. "Believe it or not, I bake when I'm stressed—if I have the time." I had more of the first, less of the latter.

"Sure, that would be great. This way there will be a few things in the case if we're able to open tomorrow. And after you're done baking, read a book. I bet you haven't done that in a while."

"Fiction?" I laughed. "Not in a long while."

Cookie made a sound that suggested she was considering something. "There are cooking supplies, but I'm not sure I have much by way of real food." Worry crept into her tone.

"I'll figure it out," I said. Worst case, I had a banana and a granola bar in my car. Under all that snow. "How's Sammie doing?" I asked, changing the subject.

"Sleeping."

"Good, she needs it." I pulled back the blinds and found Ted brushing the snow off my car just as he had promised.

"And Maddie's sleeping in too. Apparently, the school has decided not to do remote learning."

I laughed. "That must have made her happy."

"These kids spend too much time in front of screens. Let them sleep in and play in the snow."

"Ha! I doubt Maddie will be playing in the snow, but..." I

dropped the blinds and lowered myself onto the arm of the cozy chair under the window.

When I thought of the long day ahead of me, I realized I probably should have slept in too. I had hours and hours ahead of me to fill. Did I even know how to sleep in? Apparently, a lifetime of owning the bakery had also made Cookie unable to lounge around. I smiled to myself. Maddie was probably going to have a chore list as long as her arm when she woke up, making her wish they hadn't cancelled school.

"I'll be here if any of the deliveries happen to make it," I said, assuring my grandmother.

"Your sister and I are grateful."

A flush of warmth washed over me. "That's what family is for." I repeated Cookie's familiar refrain.

Softly in the background came the whistle of the tea kettle. "I taught you well. I'll give you a call later."

"Wait," I said quickly. "Who's your repair guy? The furnace in the apartment is busted. I could've baked cookies on it when I woke up, and now it seems to have quit."

Cookie let out a soft tsk. "Trevor must've forgotten to check it. He's on a new route. I worry he'll fall asleep on one of these long hauls. And now this weather…"

Her voice was full of concern, but I wasn't sure it came from a place of admiration. More likely, it was the kind of concern you reserve for someone who marries into the family and then underdelivers. Or maybe that was just me, projecting. Years of Sammie's venting had done a number on my objectivity when it came to my brother-in-law.

I let myself slide over the arm and melt into the oversized chair. My thoughts drifted to the handyman next door. Maybe Ted could fix the radiator. He was a handyman, after all.

"I'll figure something out," I said, mostly to myself.

Cookie might still chat with Big Ed, but I wasn't about to rope her into an awkward neighborhood dispute if Sammie got prickly about Ted doing odd jobs for us. Sammie could yell at me *after* I had the radiator fixed.

I ended the call and tossed my phone onto the cushion beside me, its dark screen mirroring the stillness of the house. I opened my laptop, but the Wi-Fi was out.

Maybe the world was forcing me to slow down. A feat in itself.

Since I wasn't yet up to baking, I reached for a book on the shelf, cracked the spine, and settled in. But my brain couldn't focus on the words. For all the times I'd wished my busy schedule would slow down, I hadn't realized I wouldn't know what to do with myself once it had.

emily

Baking put me in a meditative state. In college, it had been my stress-reliever, my secret weapon during finals. And, okay, it also made me wildly popular in the dorms. After graduation, baking didn't fit into the corporate climb. Long hours in finance barely afforded me time to sleep, never mind bake. And kitchens in small apartments were the worst for baking. But every minute was devoured anyway by spreadsheets, business meetings, and strategic job pivots that landed me exactly where I was determined to stay: financially independent and flexible.

I poked holes in the dough for Cookie's famous shortbread, slid the trays in the oven, and let out a breath. This kitchen was heaven. Getting into the old routine of falling into baking, forgetting all my worries, made me wonder what my life might have looked like if I hadn't set upon such a stressful career.

Shaking off the thought, I grabbed my laptop, checked my emails for anything new from Blue Moon, then fired off a request to my sister to send me the business records. She agreed without argument, probably because she was loopy from pain meds. As I scrolled through the digital files, my stomach sank. The bakery was barely breaking even. And the addition of fancy coffees wasn't going to fix that.

Not without a real plan.

Maybe my sister's accident was a blessing in disguise. Not that Sammie would ever think so. But without my coming home and going through the financials myself, I might have blindly continued to send good money after bad to prop up this business.

What choice did I have?

I pushed my laptop aside and peeked in the oven. The shortbread was turning that golden shade of "almost done," as Cookie used to say.

Resting my backside against the counter, I felt a familiar weight settle on my shoulders. This strange sense of responsibility for Sammie always snuck up on me when I was here. Maybe it didn't make logical sense because she was the older one. But when we were kids, she was the one who made me feel less alone, less awkward, less like the girl who spent most of her time babysitting and studying and calling it fun. I wouldn't be where I was if she hadn't been cheering me on even after her own path veered off course.

I rubbed the back of my neck, sensing there was something else I should be doing. That was when I spotted a bowl of apples on the counter. Ted's voice echoed in my mind. *Best apple turnovers I've ever had.*

Could I make them?

I opened and closed drawers, hunting for Cookie's ancient recipe book. Post-renovation, the kitchen had been upgraded, but the organizational system had not. The usual suspects were in a laminated binder on the counter, but no sign of the elusive turnovers.

Then I remembered my laptop. When vintage cookbooks failed, Google delivered. A five-star recipe popped up, and within minutes I was peeling apples like a woman on a mission, taking only a quick break to pull the shortbread from the oven.

I'd just chopped the last one when my email pinged. My heart did a full nosedive. I lunged for the laptop only to find it was only another alumni donation plea. My pulse resumed normal speed.

Shaking off the nerves, I set the apples aside and got to work on the dough. I flipped on the stand mixer and—*whoosh*—flour flew out of the bowl, landing squarely on my laptop.

"Fantastic," I muttered, brushing flour off the keys. I moved the laptop to a far corner of the kitchen.

I got lost in the rest of the task of rolling, filling, sealing, and brushing with egg wash. By the time the tray slid into the oven, I was beginning to understand why Cookie had phased them out. High effort, high mess. Delicious, but too much work.

With my hands still dusted in flour, I turned to the dishes, filling the sink with warm, sudsy water. It was mindless work but oddly grounding. The scent of shortbread and turnovers filled the air, wrapping around me like a memory. People used to come in just for a warm square of Cookie's short-bread. I hoped mine didn't disappoint.

I pulled the turnovers out of the oven and set them on the stainless-steel counter next to the shortbread. A sharp knock broke through the quiet. I grabbed a dish towel, drying my hands as I made my way to the front door.

And there he was. Ted. Grinning. Goofy hat and all.

We have to stop meeting like this, I thought.

Apparently, I wasn't the only one looking for something to do.

I hadn't had any in-person interaction since his early morning drop-in, so I wasn't exactly sorry to see him again. In fact, I was more than a little excited to offer him one of those turnovers. I unlocked the front door and swung it open. An arctic gust rushed in, a shock to my system.

"Come in, come in. It's freezing out there." No need to waste time before inviting him in this time.

"Oh, it smells good in here." He drew in a deep breath, filling his lungs.

I smiled, feeling a strange sense of accomplishment that had never come from sitting behind a computer screen. "I've been baking." I stated the obvious, wiping my hands on the dish towel I was holding then tossing it over my shoulder without missing a beat. I had seen Cookie do that a million times. I looked at Ted expectantly. "Cookie's shortbread." I wasn't sure why I felt compelled to surprise him with the turnovers.

He lifted a white plastic bag, the thin straps wound around his leather gloves. The most heavenly smell wafted from it. "Wasn't sure if you had anything to eat." A smile twitched the corners of his mouth. "Other than baked goods."

My stomach growled. "I haven't had much of anything. Well, anything that didn't have sugar, flour, and baking soda in it."

"Well, here you go." He extended his hand, and the bag twirled until it unwound from his gloves.

My arm dropped with the weight of the bag. "Um, I can run upstairs and grab my purse if you want to wait a minute." *I'm not sure what this is, but I don't want him to think—oh, I don't know—anything other than that I should offer to pay him.* My mother had instilled that in me too. No handouts.

He waved me off.

"I really can't accept this from you," I said.

He regarded me carefully, a smile pulling at the corners of his full mouth. "You're one stubborn woman." His eyes flashed bright. "How about we trade? You can slip me some of that shortbread when it's ready. You can have a decent dinner I whipped up."

My eyebrows shot up. "You made this?"

"Yep."

"You are a jack of all trades." I set the bag down on the table and pulled out something warm wrapped in deli paper.

"I wasn't sure what you'd like. That one..." He leaned closer to check the writing on the wrapper. The smell of cold—yes, freezing cold had a smell—and a hint of aloe from his skin mixed with the savory scent of the sandwich. "That one is turkey, tomato, and cheese, and the other is pepper, onion, and cheese. In case you are one of those people who doesn't eat meat." He shrugged and smiled in a playful I-didn't-mean-anything-by-it gesture. "Not that there's anything wrong with that." A look of concern chased the smug expression from his face. "Oops, I didn't consider a vegan option."

I laughed and shook my head. "Both sound amazing. Pretty sure I'm getting the better end of this deal." I gestured to the nearest chair, and he obligingly pulled it out for me.

"You've had Cookie's shortbread, right?" He lifted an eyebrow.

"Of course." I blinked. "Why?"

"Then we'll call it even."

"Fair enough." I sat down, feeling a little more put together in street clothes, makeup, and mostly tamed hair.

I unwrapped the other sandwich and pushed it toward him. "Want to split both?"

"Glad you asked." He grabbed half of the sandwich in front of me. "It's been so quiet. I was starting to talk to myself."

"Why not go home?" He'd said he lived nearby. Was anyone waiting for him? I didn't dare ask. It wasn't my place. And yet, the unasked question lingered on the tip of my tongue for fear I'd come off as nosy.

"I wanted to catch up on work," he said, sitting down in the chair across from mine.

"I know what you mean."

"Feel like a beer? Wine maybe? I can run next door and grab something," he said, pushing back in his chair.

"I don't want you to get in trouble."

His brow furrowed then lifted, and a small smile tugged at the corners of his mouth.

What was that all about?

I didn't want him to think he had to raid his employer's kitchen just because it was a snow day. As it was, he had brought me over food from the brewery. I'd offer him money again, but I sensed he'd be offended.

He narrowed his eyes, dragged his hand through his hair, turned away, then looked back. "It's not a problem. Have any favorites? We have fun Christmas sours."

I shook my head slowly. Our initial easy camaraderie had grown awkward. Maybe a couple of beers would chill us both out. "Sounds perfect." I forced a smile. "If you don't mind going back out into the cold."

He held up a finger and snagged his coat from the chair but left his gloves and hat on the table. "I'll be right back."

He pushed through the front door, leaving a swirl of arctic air in his wake. I quickly turned away when he caught me tracking his movements through the front window. I unpacked the other sandwich, and my stomach rumbled again.

I got up, went behind the case, grabbed some napkins, and set us up at the table, wondering what I had done to shift the mood. Maybe I should've graciously accepted the sandwiches without a fuss and sent him on his way. Instead, I'd backed myself into spending time with a ridiculously charming man who was absolutely not my type. I was playing with a fire that no amount of the snow piling up outside could extinguish.

Easy, girl. My sister's voice scraped across my mind. *He offered you a sandwich and a beer. There's no commitment in that.* Sammie always told me I was too serious about everything. That I had grown old before my time.

I ran a finger under one of my eyes then the other before

yanking out the elastic that I had put in my hair to keep it out of my baking and did a quick fluff.

Who am I trying to impress?

Traitorous butterflies stirred in my stomach as if they'd caught wind of my wandering thoughts. Before I could get too swept away in my own romantic daydream, I figured I better check on the baked goods. The golden shortbread had cooled on the steel counter. Next to them sat the turnovers. I leaned in and drew a deep breath, and the warm, spiced scent hit me square in the face. My stomach growled. Everything smelled incredible.

I ran to the small customer bathroom off the dining room and checked my reflection. Phew, nothing on my face that didn't belong.

My phone vibrated in my back pocket. I slipped it out. *Sammie.* As if I had conjured her up with my thoughts. I swiped my finger across the screen. "Hey there. How are you?"

"How are *you*? Are you going stir crazy?"

"I'm fine. I made a few batches of shortbread and decided to try those apple turnovers Cookie used to make." I stared at myself in the mirror, raking my fingers through my hair, tucking it behind my ear, then immediately untucking it.

Oh no. Am I primping for a date?

"Impressive," Sammie said. "What made you think of those? I can't remember the last time we had them."

I pictured her curled up on the couch, knees pulled to her chest, chin resting on top, then I remembered the sprained ankle and mentally swapped her pose to something more horizontal.

"Oh, I don't know," I said, which was a lie. A certain flannel-wearing handyman had dropped a not-so-subtle hint. But if I mentioned him in any context other than the handyman next door, Sammie would zero in like a rom-com bloodhound. Oh, she loved me unconditionally but especially when she had something juicy to tease me about.

Wow. I've definitely been cooped up too long.

Even before my return to Walleye Point, work had bull-dozed my personal life into submission. I honestly couldn't remember the last time I'd been on a real date.

"Thanks. Saves me from having to bake," Sammie said, yanking me out of my thoughts.

"With your broken wrist?" I said, deadpan.

"There is that." Her tone had softened, had became distant. Almost wistful.

"Are your suppliers going to be able to get in tomorrow?" I asked. "I imagine your regulars are going to want something other than shortbread and turnovers to go with their coffee."

Sammie sighed heavily. "Are you planning on being the barista too?"

"I can handle basic coffee. People will understand."

"One of the girls who was a pro at making specialty drinks left last week," she said, as if answering the question on my mind. "Well, she was mostly only weekends, but bad timing, I know. Cookie could run the bakery in a pinch, but she has no interest in the coffee part of the shop."

Hearing the strain in her voice, I said, "I'm here if the deliveries make it. I can offer black coffee and the basics. I'll push through."

"You always do." The evenness of Sammie's comment wasn't meant to jab, but it still hit that old nerve that was directly wired to my twelve-year-old self. The one so eager to please my big sister.

I shoved the uneasy feeling aside. Why did I let these little things nag at me? I knew better. It wasn't about her tone or the words. It was about me, and the way certain memories clung tighter than I'd like to admit.

"If it keeps snowing, it'll probably be quiet tomorrow too," I said, trying to still my rioting thoughts.

Sammie sighed again. "This doesn't bode well for the holiday season."

"It's early in the month." I slid out of the bathroom, trying to sound reassuring. "We'll get this place humming."

"Ugh, this is absolutely the worst time for me to be laid up."

"I'd wager that there's no good time for that." I chuckled at my sister's expense.

It was refreshing to hear my big sister laugh. "Bonus, I binge-watched all of *Yellowstone, 1883,* and *1923.*"

I glanced toward the front door. Still no sign of Ted. "Hey, did you have any plans to decorate the storefront?" I decided to ask about this instead of addressing her financials. That should probably be dealt with face-to-face. Even still, I probably should have asked about the decorations, too, before I ordered a bunch of stuff online.

"You saw the flyer."

"Yeah," I said, careful to keep my tone even. "I was bored, so I ordered a few things online, *and* I found someone to put them up."

"Okay, cool. Yeah, I hadn't gotten around to it. With everything else going on." Sammie's tone had gone flat. Perhaps I had stepped on her toes. "Wait, you hired someone?"

"The handyman from Top Shelf." My heart rate spiked, as if I expected to be scolded. *Good grief, I'm a grown woman.* "I saw him putting up their decorations before the storm. So I asked him if he wanted another job."

"Yesterday?"

"Yeah, he—"

"Are you serious?" My sister interrupted me, humor mixed with disbelief in her voice. "The handyman who was hanging the lights on the front of the brewery?" The way she bit out the last word confirmed that hiring someone from the business next door was a bad idea.

A wave of heat washed over me. "It seemed like the most efficient way to—"

Sammie interrupted me. "Just to be clear, what did he look like?"

I sat down, watching the door for the man with piercing brown eyes; a chiseled, whiskered jaw; and a broad chest. But I kept that description to myself. "He wears this goofy hat with side flaps."

Sammie sighed, and I sensed she was covering her face with her palm. "That man is Ted Hemsley. He owns the brewery."

"What?" My pulse roared in my ears as Ted came into view. He cheerfully lifted a six-pack of beer when he walked through the door. I held up my finger and mouthed "Hold on." He set the beer on the table then shrugged out of his coat. His brown hair, cut neat at the sides and longer on top, had been whipped into a tousled mess by the wind. The kind of hair that I would have loved to run my fingers through.

Cheeks growing hot, I tapped the screen, taking my phone off speaker. *What the heck is wrong with me?*

"You asked Ted to do handyman tasks around *my* bakery," Sammie said, enunciating each word as if she was reading some shocking headline from the news. Honestly, I couldn't tell if she was mad, amused, or perhaps delighted that she caught me in a moment of questionable judgment.

"I thought…" I whispered into the phone, painfully aware that Ted was still standing behind me. And that he'd heard every single word before I'd finally remembered how to turn off the speakerphone.

"I promise, Ted's not the handyman. He took over the business after his father died."

My stomach dropped like it had missed a step.

Ted. Owned. The brewery.

The same brewery that had driven Mrs. Davis and her flower shop out. The one that nearly strong-armed Cookie and Sammie into selling. The one I'd basically paid to keep at bay.

"Oh..." My pulse roared in my ears as I turned to face him. Ted Hemsley. Of course. One brow raised and that stupidly handsome, maddeningly smug smile playing at the edges of his mouth. He had made himself at home in the seat across from me.

"Can I call you back later?" I asked, not breaking eye contact with Ted.

"Sure. Everything okay?" Sammie said.

"Yeah." I hung up.

Perfectly okay. If you ignored the fact that I'd spent the last twenty-four hours flirting with the enemy.

Gosh darn it.

Just my luck he's so ridiculously good-looking.

8 /

ted

I grabbed a beer, twisted off the cap, and took a long swig, mostly to hide the grin I couldn't quite contain. Emily had been quick to take the phone off speaker, but I caught the gist. I guessed I didn't have to figure out how to work that little reveal into the conversation.

"Can I call you back later?" she said into the phone before wrapping up the call.

She cleared her throat, her face noticeably paler than before. "I thought you were the handyman."

I pointed at her with my beer. "To be fair, I never said I was the handyman."

Emily shook her head slowly then dropped back into her seat, snagging a beer from the table. With the sleeve of her sweater pulled over the bottle, she twisted off the cap, took a long swig, then swiped the same sleeve across her mouth.

"Why would you let me go on and on about hiring you for odd projects?" she asked.

I leaned back, hooking my arm over the chair like I had all the time in the world. "Why not?"

I was enjoying this way too much. Emily used to have a great sense of humor—before life and adulthood had done their thing. Yet, how could she hold any of this against me? I was more than willing to put up their decorations even if I was more than handy with tools. And I had brought her food and beer in the middle of a snowstorm. That had to count for something.

The sharpness of her eyes made me rethink my lie of omission. "Listen, I never intended to deceive you. You just… made the leap to handyman. I just so happen to also be part owner of the brewery." And it was clear from her initial reaction that she didn't remember me as a teen. I wanted to believe it was because I didn't go by the name Ted back then and not because I was so forgettable.

Leaning forward, I rested my elbows on the table, closing the space between us just enough to make it interesting and to ground myself in the moment, not the past. "It's not unheard of for an owner to do actual physical labor. We're not some big-time operation."

Her eyes narrowed. "The brewery tried to force the sale of the bakery."

Ah. There it was.

She wasn't about to let me off the hook that easily.

I jerked my head back. "We were hoping to use the lot for parking."

"So, you were going to tear our building down."

"We tore down the floral shop in the expansion." I scratched my head, feeling defensive on behalf of Dad. "It's business. My dad put everything into it." *Everything.* Including his health. His life.

Color infused her cheeks, and she bowed her head, as if the mention of my deceased father had shifted the mood. "I'm sorry about your dad."

"Yeah, me too." My voice cracked. My father's death at the prime of his life had left a lot of unfinished business, business I felt compelled to complete.

"Listen, I don't mean to speak ill of the dead," Emily said, interrupting my thoughts, "but I suspect there were a lot of…" She seemed to be choosing her words carefully. "Unfortunate things that occurred that made Mrs. Davis sell her shop. The bakery also had to sink a lot of money into fines and improvements. I personally fronted the money. Otherwise, you might be parking your truck right where we're sitting."

"I'm not sure how all that played out," I said, unable to keep the defensiveness from my voice. It was true. My dad had had a lot of balls in the air when I got the frantic call from Galina that Ed had been rushed to the hospital. "We were weeks away from opening when I came back to help out. My stepmom, Galina, was at wit's end. The business probably would have folded before it even got off the ground if I hadn't stepped in." I tipped my head in the direction of the brewery. "If I hadn't, you might have a big empty husk of a building next door. Where would that leave you? A rising tide lifts all boats and all that, right?" I ran a hand across my jaw. "I'm proud of what I did to honor my father's memory. His dream."

A small smile graced her pretty lips. "I get that, I do. But my sister is doing her best to have a successful business too." She dragged a hand through her hair. Her somber tone made me wonder if there was more to this. "An empty building wouldn't be taking up all the parking spots."

"Or you could argue that people wouldn't bother coming down Main Street if it looked like a ghost town."

Emily cocked her head. "You never got your parking, so it leaves me to wonder if a surprise health department inspection was a coincidence."

I held out my hand. "You think we had something to do with that?" My heart thudded slowly, considering what she was telling me. Turning over all options, I recalled how stressed my father had been while opening the brewery. How he'd outright claimed he'd remove *any* roadblocks. I'd chalked it up to my father's never-say-die attitude, the same spirit that pushed me in sports as a kid. My father had been stern and demanding, but he was ethical.

"Your father is gone. It's all in the past." She leaned back hard in the chair, her lips pressed into a thin line.

"No, tell me. I want to know how your business was affected," I said, feeling like some of the air had been sucked out of the room.

Emily leaned forward again and folded the edge of the deli paper from our subs. They were getting cold, but it seemed like neither of us was hungry anymore.

"Excluding forcing Mrs. Davis out of business, someone filed complaints with the New York State Department of Health. I paid for a complete kitchen remodel to make sure it complied with all the codes, even though the original one was perfectly fine."

Emily spat out the last word, and I realized why my father had been unsuccessful in taking over the bakery. His grand plans had been to expand the brewery to take up the entire city block, including parking. His plans had been bold and expensive. "Isn't it a good thing the bakery is up to code?" The need to defend my father was strong.

"It was up to code," Emily said, "but fighting with the health department seemed like an expensive proposition when we could use the money for improvements. My sister was stressed that they'd keep finding something. Keep nitpicking. We thought brand-new upgrades would shut them up for good. Then the building was reappraised, and the taxes went up. More money I had to come up with. I bought the building, removing that stress from my sister. The way things unfolded was slick and underhanded. Your family has a lot of friends on the town council." She held out her palms. "This was my grandmother's and sister's livelihood. It *is* their livelihood." She collapsed back into her chair once more and picked at the label on her beer bottle, seemingly deep in thought.

"My father wouldn't have done that." My heart pounded, stubborn in its defense. He was a man of principles, even if he hadn't always shown them in the smoothest way.

Emily looked up at me, guarded now. "I'm not here to speak ill of your dad. But I do have concerns—real ones—that your business is still trying to lay claim to our space."

It wasn't fire in her voice, exactly. No, it was more like the steel of a woman who had no problem drawing lines.

"We're not," I said, fast, wanting her to hear me clearly. "That's not what this is." I hesitated. "Look, if you told me tomorrow you wanted to sell, we'd make an offer. No question. We need the parking. That's not a secret."

Her lips twitched, barely. "Keep circling the block, buddy." There it was, that spark of humor. Then, just as quickly, it was gone. Replaced with something quieter. "This bakery means everything to my sister. To my whole family."

"Then you get it," I said. "That's why I'm here too. This business is part of my family's legacy. I'm trying to make sure it still supports us."

"Okay," she said softly. "Then maybe it's best if we keep things separate." I wasn't sure what she meant by that until she said, "I'll find someone else to hang our decorations."

"Whatever you need to do." I stood, feeling defensive. "I'll let you eat."

She gave a faint smile, polite but distant. "Thanks again. For the sandwiches."

"You're welcome." I grabbed my coat and stuffed my arms into it.

"Hold up," she said, as if suddenly remembering something. She hustled to the back then returned with a white bakery box. "As promised. Dessert."

We locked our full attention on one another. I wasn't sure what to make of this, then she said, "My end of the agreement."

"Of course. Thanks." I couldn't help but feel disappointment over an evening that had started out so promising. But it had all been under false pretenses before she knew I was the co-owner of the business next door. That alone had probably canceled out whatever goodwill I'd built over bar food and free labor.

Yet she still didn't remember me from before. When we were teens.

And maybe that was for the best.

Because whatever she thought of me now...

It definitely wasn't *good*.

9 /
ted

I drove the few blocks home, the winter air sharp, the roads slick, and Emily Johnson's accusations lodged firmly in my brain.

Had my dad—big football star, small-town hero, lifelong member of the good ol' boys club—pulled strings to get what he wanted? And when the last obstacle standing in his way was the bakery's land, had he tried to force them out?

Turned out, Emily had been the one to stop him.

I scrubbed a hand across my face as I approached the unplowed driveway of my childhood home. I parked along the curb, or somewhere in the proximity of it. Trudging up the driveway, I figured I'd have to grab the snowblower from the garage to clear out the driveway. Most businesses should be open by tomorrow, and Galina and Gramps would need their cars dug out.

I wandered into the darkened living room. What little light there was came from the flickering TV. Big Ed was dozing in his chair, and Jayden was on the couch, hunched over his phone. The house smelled faintly of dinner.

"Do you remember how to work that snowblower?" I asked my nephew.

"Yeah," he muttered, not looking up.

"Then how come we have two feet of snow in the driveway?"

Jayden tipped his head back to rest on the couch. "It's still snowing, dude."

"By that theory, I should wait until winter's over because it might snow again."

"Don't be a drama king. I had something to check on my phone."

Big Ed stirred from his slumber. He planted his hands on the arms of his worn chair and made to get up. "Ah, you're home. I meant to get out there and shovel a path."

I chuckled. "You shouldn't be shoveling. On the other hand…" I tipped my head to the healthy, almost-sixteen-year-old sitting on the couch. "This kid…"

"Geez!" Jayden tossed his phone down on the couch—apparently for dramatic effect because he immediately snatched it up—and stomped out of the room. "I'll do it now."

Big Ed and I exchanged a conspiratorial smile as Jayden thudded around the mudroom digging out his winter gear. His histrionics were punctuated by a slamming of the back door.

"You should go easy on the kid," Big Ed said, reaching over and fumbling with the light switch to turn on the lamp. "He's had a tough life."

I scratched my head and flopped down on the couch. "Yeah, but he also needs to take responsibility. Otherwise…"

"He might end up like his mom?" Big Ed said, dipping his head so I could see his discerning gaze under the lampshade.

"I wasn't going to say that," I said. "But that kid needs to get a fire under his butt." The words held a whisper of a memory.

Big Ed frowned. "You're sounding like your dad."

"Second time today someone suggested the apple didn't

fall far from the tree." Emily's accusatory gaze raked across my memory.

"Oh?"

"Yeah, Cookie's younger granddaughter is running the bakery while Sammie recovers from her skiing accident. Emily's staying in the apartment above the shop."

"Cookie mentioned it. She's thrilled to have her in town." Big Ed grabbed the TV remote from the table next to him and muted it. "She was worried she'd have to be in the bakery twenty-four seven when she was finally settling into retirement."

"I can't say the same for Emily. She seems resentful." I wasn't really sure why I said that. Maybe I was projecting my own feelings onto our exchange.

"It's only temporary. She has a big job offer waiting for her in Pittsburgh."

My ears perked up. A big job, huh? Cookie and Big Ed had been friends for over fifty years and had risen above the business drama between the brewery and bakery, perhaps allowing the next generation to figure it out on their own terms. Cookie seemed to be chatty when it came to her grand-daughters. Would it be so bad if I used this relationship to find out more about Emily?

"What kind of work does she do?" She seemed to have unlimited resources to bail the bakery out despite her young age.

"She has some fancy job in finance." He patted the arm of his chair. "Cookie's proud of her. The company gave her a corner office, a company credit card, and bonuses bigger than most people's salaries."

Now the image of Emily pulling up in her fancy BMW and popping out in her high-end fashion made complete sense. It was, however, in stark contrast to the fresh-faced woman I had caught off guard this morning.

"Would be nice not to have to worry about money," my

grandfather said, "but I think I'd be bored out of my mind sitting behind a computer all day."

I wasn't convinced Emily did sit behind her computer all day. But a job like hers was completely foreign to most people. Including me. I preferred to work with my hands, doing things around the brewery. All the paperwork was a necessary evil. "I tend to agree with you." I chuckled to myself. "Emily mistook me for a handyman around the brewery and asked if I could hang lights outside the bakery."

Big Ed lifted a bushy eyebrow. "Ah, competition for the best-decorated storefront." He waggled his finger at me. "Galina won't be happy. She was already grumbling that the storm delayed your getting everything up." Dad's widow had meticulously planned their decorations, even stepping it up from last year's award-winning display. She claimed that the added advertisement via the billboard on the 90 had put the brewery on the map. Like me, it was her mission to keep Dad's dream alive.

I suspected part of it had been nostalgic, maybe a little superstitious. My dad had ordered a bunch of decorations for the front of the store right before he got sick, even though it was still spring. The brewery won, and when the billboard went up the following year, the increase in business had been noticeable.

"I didn't say I'd do it," I said.

Big Ed shrugged, apropos of nothing. He was the best man I knew. His devotion to work and family was admirable. He leaned closer and whispered, "I won't tell if you want to help Cookie's granddaughter out."

"Galina would find out. She misses nothing," I whispered.

"What will *she* find out?" Galina walked into the living room as if on cue. She had a paperback in one hand and a teacup in the other. She was probably coming down from her bedroom for a refill.

I rubbed my neck. "Sammie's sister asked me if I'd put Christmas decorations up for them."

"Why would she ask you?"

"She thought I was a handyman."

"Odd." Galina pursed her lips, as if considering. "I thought maybe Sammie's accident would be the kick in the pants she needed to realize running a business didn't stop for anything."

Harsh turn of phrase, but I kept my mouth shut.

"Maybe the business-savvy sister will talk some sense into Sammie," Galina said, never one to miss an opportunity to give the older Johnson sister a jab.

I held up my hands, not wanting to wade into that discussion, and Galina disappeared upstairs, out of earshot.

"She needs to accept we won't secure that property for parking," I said. "Emily is not interested in selling." Emily's steely gaze flashed in my memory.

"You never know. You said she seemed resentful. Maybe she'll convince Sammie that small-town business isn't for everyone. People are allowed to change their minds."

"They are." But I didn't think she would. I had grown weary of this conversation and wanted to get outside and snowplow, to lose myself in physical labor. Based on the silence, Jayden hadn't started up the machine yet.

"It seems that you and Emily have that in common. You both stepped in when your families needed you." Big Ed's voice cracked. "We were all so grateful you came home when Ed got sick that we didn't consider if it was the best thing for you." He cleared his throat. "We're really glad you're here."

Uncomfortable with the emotional confession, I stood and tapped the back of Big Ed's chair as I passed. "Happy to be here too. I was ready for a change." There was some truth to that. I had left Walleye Point for college and gotten a job in sales. I was doing pretty well when Dad got sick. But I was bored as heck. I needed a change. I hadn't planned on running a brewery, though. *Yet here we are.*

The sound of metal scraping against cement pulled our attention to the front of the house.

Jayden was out there, shoveling. The snowblower was tricky to start.

"And don't be too hard on the kid," my grandfather said. "He's a good one."

My chest tightened. On top of the mantel sat two high school portraits. My sister's bright and carefree smile gave no indication of the darkness that would swallow her whole. No sign of the choices that would cost her custody of her son.

I had returned for my dad.

I had stayed for Jayden.

When my sister lost custody, my dad and Galina took him in. For the first time, he had a stable home. And then, just as quickly, that was ripped from him too. I'd made peace that I'd be here until Jayden left for college. That much, I had prepared for.

What I hadn't prepared for—not in a million years—was seeing the girl who broke my heart at sixteen walk back into my life.

10 /
emily

It was beginning to feel a bit like *Groundhog Day* as I climbed out of bed and found myself staring over the snowy, sleepy town. The plows had cleared the streets down to the pavement, and a few cars were making their way down Main Street. Releasing a long breath, I hugged my hoodie to my sides and realized I had better get ready for the day. The earliest delivery was in less than an hour.

My sleep had been fitful, my mind replaying bits and pieces of the conversation I had had with Ted. Wondering if I said the wrong thing and feeling like he was holding back. Was he angry at my family for stifling his father's dream? For creating stress? Yet I had every right to point fingers right back at him. His family had tried to force my sister's bakery out of business.

He shouldn't get a pass for that.

Yet I felt like something more was going on behind those mesmerizing eyes. Perhaps what I mistook for romantic interest was merely curiosity. I was simply a new face in town. An outsider.

Shrugging away my spiraling thoughts, I quickly made the bed, freshened up for the day, and headed downstairs. Before I reached the bottom of the staircase, I heard a commotion at the back door. It sounded like someone was struggling. I paused for a beat before rushing the rest of the way down the stairs.

With my heart thundering in my ears, I pressed against the steel door leading out to the alleyway to listen. The voice was familiar, but I was still cautious. "Hey, Sammie, is that you?" I asked through the closed door.

"Who else would it be, Einstein?" The thick door did nothing to muffle the annoyance in my big sister's voice.

I quickly twisted the lock and yanked the door open. Sammie lurched forward with her key stuck in the lock, a crutch tucked under her armpit. I reached out and righted her.

"Oh my goodness, what are you doing? You should be home resting." I stuck out my lower lip and blew away the hair that had fallen into my eyes.

"I brought Trevor to look at the heating in the apartment." Her words came out clipped, as if it were my fault the radiator alternated between sauna and Siberia. She limped inside, and the steel door slammed sharply and cut off the wind whipping down the back alley. I let my hand hover near her elbow, ready to rescue her if the crutch slipped. Apparently, she had traded in the knee scooter.

Sammie jerked her head toward the door. "Can you open the door for Trev?"

"Oh, sure."

Clutching my hoodie closed at the neck, I pulled open the door in time to find Trevor closing the tailgate of his truck with unnecessary force, then he shuffle-stepped along the narrow space between the truck and the back wall of the bakery, jostling a red toolbox.

"Hey, kid," he muttered as he passed, the solid door slamming behind him. I got the distinct feeling he would've tousled my hair if he hadn't been in a hurry to get inside. In his eyes, I'd always been Sammie's kid sister, the tagalong at summer bonfires and late-night ice cream runs.

"Thanks, Trevor. It's the radiator under the window. It's either on full steam or not at all."

He gave me a casual salute and trudged up the back stairs to my apartment.

I raised my eyebrows then quickly schooled my expression. Sammie and Trevor were a whole mood this morning. Most of what I knew about him came from my sister's venting sessions, not from spending actual time with the guy. Whenever I visited, he always seemed busy. Watching the Bills. Or grabbing beers with his high school crew. When Sammie hitched her wagon to his after their surprise pregnancy, it always felt like her life pivoted while his just coasted along the same track it had always been on.

"Did he get up on the wrong side of the bed?" I asked, immediately regretting it. I needed to be grateful. The man was fixing the radiator. That was more than I could say for the handsome neighbor I had mistaken for the handyman. My cheeks warmed at the memory. Definitely not the handyman.

"Trevor's just tired," Sammie said, as if she needed to excuse her husband's attitude.

"You must be tired too," I said gently.

"You have no idea." She gave a little hop on her good foot, wobbling as she adjusted her crutch.

"Come on. Let's go sit."

I slowed my pace to match hers, hovering close to catch her if she stumbled. At the front of the bakery, she eased into a chair with a long sigh. Her crutch slipped from her grasp and clattered to the floor with a sharp thwack.

I bent to retrieve it, but she waved me off. "Leave it. I'll grab it when I go."

"Coffee?"

Sammie shook her head. "No, no. I'm fine." She sniffed.

"Let's keep the store closed today. I don't think many people will be out in this weather."

"No deliveries?"

"No. I called all of the suppliers." She must've done it right after Cookie ran through the schedule with me. "They were glad to hear from me. Everyone's still scrambling after the storm. They'll have us back on the route tomorrow morning." She lifted an eyebrow. "That work for you?"

"Yeah, no problem," I said. "I can do paperwork today. Get organized."

Sammie groaned like doing paperwork was like a poker to the eye. "The paperwork part is the worst. Maybe you could help me figure out a system, so it's not such a pain?" She met my gaze knowingly. This was a huge step.

A flutter of excitement rose in my chest. This was something I was good at. Something more useful than handing over a check. I knew she appreciated the financial help, but part of her chafed at what felt like charity. She wanted to stand on her own, and I got that.

"I went through a few files yesterday," I said. "I'd love to help streamline everything."

She released a long sigh and sank back into the chair. "Do you think I got in over my head with this?"

"The bakery?" I asked.

She nodded. "Buying the bakery from Cookie seemed like the most logical thing to do. It's what I know." She gave a half-hearted shrug then made a move for her crutch before giving up. "It's not like I'm qualified to do anything else."

I traced the edge of the table with my fingertip, choosing my words like I was walking a tightrope. We'd had a thousand conversations about her being a good mom, about Cookie aging, about our mom working herself into the ground, and Trevor being Trevor. But she'd never said she wasn't sure about the bakery. I always assumed this was her dream.

"You don't have to keep doing this," I said gently. "If it's not what you want." The thought of shutting down the place Cookie had poured her soul into stung, but not as much as the idea of Sammie feeling trapped. "You could go back to school. I could help with tuition."

Sammie picked at a fraying edge on her cast then gave a little head shake like she was trying to clear the fog. "I'm just wallowing. That black diamond trail was a dumb risk."

I reached across and touched her hand. "Let me help you set up the books so it's not such a beast. I love doing that stuff." At my job, I was so far removed from the customer it was all spreadsheets and projections. Useful, sure, but not exactly soul-satisfying.

"You're such a geek," Sammie said, brushing a hand across her cheek.

"Guilty." I tapped her fingers and pulled back, the wheels in my brain already turning. For now, we had a plan. And that felt good.

"How did things go yesterday with your little handyman buddy?" Sammie leaned heavily into mock-little-sister mode, clearly wanting to change the subject.

A flood of heat rushed up my cheeks at the memory of learning Ted owned the brewery. Co-owned. Whatever. "I am such an idiot for not putting two and two together much sooner."

Sammie hugged her broken arm and played with the edge of her cast, wincing. "That surprises me."

I dragged a hand through my hair. "That I can be an idiot sometimes?"

A sly smile replaced the smug one on Sammie's face. "He's pretty hot, though, right?" She turned around to make sure Trevor wasn't within hearing distance.

I pressed my lips together tighter, unable to hold back a laugh. "Um, yes."

Sammie playfully pointed at me. "Ah, you should go for it."

I rolled my eyes. "I can't date public enemy number one." *Can I?*

Sammie lifted a shoulder. "It was his father who was the pain in the butt. May he rest in peace," she muttered as an afterthought, probably mimicking something Cookie would say. "And his widow is a piece of work. Galina won't let things go. I kinda think that Ted's just going along to keep the peace."

I shook my head. I hadn't carved out a career in finance by blindly trusting everyone. Still, brushing off my sister wouldn't win me any points. Despite the different worlds we inhabited, she had always had my best interests at heart. "It doesn't matter. I'm not looking to date anyone. My career is my focus."

"Your career won't keep you warm at night," Sammie said, eyeing me so hard I felt like squirming under her stare. I never should have shared that my dating life sucked.

I rubbed the back of my neck. "I have a faulty radiator for that." I smirked.

Sammie pointed to the ceiling, indicating Trevor upstairs. "Not for long." She flattened her hand on the table. "You're not getting any younger."

"Any younger for what? I have everything I've ever wanted." Money, security, and independence. All things our mom had drilled into our heads.

Sammie shrugged. "You let Mom brainwash you." Apparently, she could also read my mind.

"She was only looking out for us."

"I'll give her that." Sammie leaned back. "Our dad really did a number on her. She was determined we'd stand on our own two feet." She gave a half laugh. "She wanted to kill me when I got pregnant at eighteen."

I watched her profile as she stared out the front window,

her expression unreadable. "Maddie turned out to be a pretty great prize, all things considered."

That softened her. Sammie turned to me with a wistful smile. "She is a good kid, isn't she?"

"The best."

She took in a deep breath and gave me a sideways look. "You should really consider having a fling with Ted."

I groaned. "We're back to that?"

"What's the harm in it? Have a little fun, then off you go to your shiny new job in January."

"Exactly why it's a terrible idea." Ted looked like the kind of man who would break my heart. "And let's not forget, he admitted he'd bulldoze the bakery for a parking lot if he had the chance." I left out the nuance. He hadn't actually said it with malice, just matter-of-fact honesty. But it felt good to say it out loud. Like drawing a line in the snow and daring myself not to cross it.

Sammie jerked her head back, a flash of surprise crossing her features. "I suppose business is business." She drummed her hands on the table. "Speaking of the storefront."

"Were we?" I joked. "Ah, yes, the decorations."

"Yeah, that too. But I think we need a better name than Bakery. Maybe you can brainstorm a few when you're bored."

"Have any in mind?"

"Maddie is having fun with it. Ideas like Rolling in Dough, Cookie's Crumbs, Butter Late than Never." She held out her hand. "I could go on all day."

"And you still haven't landed on one?" I laughed. "I don't understand why not."

"I'll know it when I hear it."

A thud sounded upstairs followed by the deep rumble of someone having a bad morning. "Sounds like Trevor is having problems," I said.

Sammie drew in a deep breath and let it go without responding. Not wanting to veer into one of her venting sessions about Trevor, I asked, "How's Cookie been?" I had seen her for myself, but since she was staying at Sammie's while having renovations done on her new home, I hoped to gather some insight.

Sammie's eyes grew wide as if she were bursting with juicy gossip. "I had no idea how much time she spent talking to Big Ed. I mean, sure they'd chitchat when he came in for a donut, or he'd stop by when she was baking, but they talk nonstop."

"Hmm..." I said, secretly pleased that Cookie was building an entire life separate from the bakery. Her new house. Deepening relationships.

Maybe I should have tried to get away from my one-dimensional life.

"They FaceTime late into the night," Trevor said, appearing behind us and holding his toolbox. "It's like having two teenagers in the house."

Sammie shifted in her seat to look up at her husband and waited expectantly.

"You should be able to adjust the heat now," he said.

"Thanks, I appreciate it."

He tapped the side of the toolbox. "I'm going to load up then make some calls in my truck. Come out whenever you're ready," he said to Sammie.

"Okay." Sammie twisted around in her seat. "I should probably get home. I told Maddie we could have a movie marathon today."

"You're lucky you guys are so close."

"I really am. I'm also trying to keep her distracted. Girls are rough at that age. Remember?"

"Do I ever," I grumbled. "Is she having friend trouble?"

"Yes, something to do with the cheerleading squad. I think one of the girls made alternate and is taking it out on Maddie, and Maddie's mad at me because I told her she'd need to help you at the bakery during the holidays. And it might keep her from hanging out with Jayden too much. Apparently, I am an evil mother."

"Jayden?" I had never met him in person.

"Yeah, he's Ted's nephew. He gets off the bus with Maddie," Sammie said.

Ahhh… the cool kid decked out in Walleye Point High School athletic gear, paying a lot of attention to my niece. That tracks.

"I'm not ready for my kid to start dating," she said, rubbing her forehead, as if the thought was unimaginable.

"Maddie's got her head screwed on straight," I said, defending my sweet niece.

"Everyone thought I had my head on straight." The ominous edge to her tone was unmistakable.

"You can't keep her away from boys forever."

"This one makes me nervous."

I bit my lip, giving my sister room to continue.

"He's had a rough upbringing." Her cheeks grew pink, as if she recognized she wasn't being fair. "Mr. Hemsley and his wife took him in a couple of years ago. His mom's been battling drug problems. She left town with some sketchy guy and never came back."

"That's heartbreaking," I said. "But I still don't get it. How is any of that Jayden's fault?"

"I know, I know. Poor kid." Sammie rubbed the back of her neck. "When he first transferred to Walleye Point in the middle of eighth grade, he got in a lot of trouble." She pressed her lips together. "I just think it's best if Maddie steers clear." She rolled her eyes. "Maybe I'm more like Mom than I like to admit."

"We all want what's best for our kids." My mind drifted to that good-looking kid getting off the bus with my niece. He seemed like he didn't have a care in the world. You never really knew what was going on in someone's personal life. "Galina is taking care of Jayden now that Mr. Hemsley's gone?"

My sister raised her eyebrows suddenly, as if she had even bigger dirt. "No, that's the thing. Galina's young. I mean, yeah, she pitches in, but it's Ted who is really stepping up."

"You mean, Ted is raising Jayden?"

Sammie nodded, her eyes growing wide for emphasis. "He's taken a big role. According to Big Ed—I told you Cookie and her 'friend' talk all the time—Ted filed for legal custody."

"Wow." Ted seemed so darned carefree. Not a care in the world. Who knew he was his nephew's legal guardian? Maybe I had judged him too harshly. "I had no idea all this was going on. How can I help? With Maddie," I said for clarification.

A slow smile curved my big sister's mouth. "You are helping."

"I feel bad..." Maddie was probably catching it from all sides for spending time with Jayden.

"She'll survive. We did." Sammie traced a fingertip along the edge of the table as if she were thinking of herself at that age. "She needs responsibility. I told her she needs to put in more hours at the bakery."

"I'm around too." Maddie had after-school activities she wanted to do. Sammie and I never could do those things because they required rides and money, something our single mom had trouble providing.

When I didn't say anything more, my sister leaned over and picked up her crutch from the ground. "I'll get out of your hair."

I stood and went around to help her hobble to the back of the store. "Hey wait, take some of the apple turnovers I made." When I realized she couldn't juggle them, I said, "I'll walk you out."

Trevor didn't even look up from his phone when we squeezed between the brick wall and his truck to open the door for my sister. She paused and leaned in to give me a kiss on the cheek. I helped her up into her seat and handed her the bakery box.

"Thanks for everything, Emily." She smiled, but there was a sadness in her eyes. "I'll call you later."

I shut the door gently and gave a small wave. Whether Trevor noticed or not, I couldn't tell. The cold bit at my face as I turned back toward the bakery. I darted inside and pulled the door closed behind me, grateful for the blast of warm air.

I needed structure. Checklists. Tasks I could finish and file away.

It was everything unspoken, unsettled, that always left me on edge.

11 /
emily

The storm had passed, the snowbanks shrinking under a *so-called* warm spell—by Western New York standards—and according to Cookie, business was back to normal.

Which was its own kind of problem.

Because "normal" wasn't enough to keep this place afloat.

Nearly a week of working in the bakery had only confirmed my fears—messy books, inconsistent record-keeping, and a profit margin thinner than a sheet of phyllo dough. But maybe I shouldn't leap to conclusions after only one week.

At least, that was what I told myself.

I did have something to look forward to, though. Maddie was coming straight to the bakery after school. It was the first afternoon that week she didn't have cheerleading. Technically, she could've gone home, but she said she wanted to help at the bakery. My auntie radar told a different story. It probably had more to do with Jayden, who also rode the bus to his uncle's brewery.

The diesel rumble of the school bus drew my attention to the street outside the window. I hung back so Maddie wouldn't see me spying as she and Jayden got off the bus. She turned to face him, gesturing excitedly with her hands. What I had read as overconfidence in the young man didn't come off that way today. He dipped his head and tapped the toe of his sneaker on the concrete, smashing up some ice.

Oh, I'll be… he's smitten with her.

Perhaps her mother did have reason to worry.

I could only hear muffled voices through the window. Maddie finally gave a cheerful wave and spun around on her heel. Her lashes brushed against her rosy cheeks, and a grin lit up her entire face. An expression so pure it stirred something soft and fluttery in my chest.

I darted behind the refrigerated dessert case, pretending to be deeply invested in making Maddie a mocha, her favorite, because I didn't dare get caught spying.

The sound of street noise swelled then cut off as the front door opened then swung shut behind my niece.

"Hey, Aunt Emily!"

I held down on the stainless-steel lever and twisted to greet her. I was really starting to get the hang of the fancy coffee machine. "Hey, yourself. How was school?"

My niece's long brown hair, plaited in two neat braids, poked out from under a pink Carhartt cap. "Okay."

I tracked Maddie as she dropped her school bag at one of the tables and disappeared into the bathroom to wash her hands. She still wore that goofy smile.

When she returned, she helped herself to a pastry heart from the case and slid into the seat across from me. "Have you made any more of those apple turnovers?"

"Did you try one?" I asked, brightening. I'd sent a batch home with Sammie but hadn't saved any for myself.

"Yeah," Maddie said, mid-chew. "I think you forgot a step."

My stomach dropped. "What? They weren't good?"

She glanced up, her cheeks pinking. "Sorry, Aunt Emily, but they were kinda hard. Mom said you probably forgot to cook the apples first."

I laughed, even though I died a little inside. I had given some of those turnovers to Ted. *Fabulous.* He probably thought I was a horrible baker, and I wasn't sure why it bothered me so much.

"Well," I said, trying to sound breezy, "good to know. I'll read the directions more carefully next time." Strange, I thought I had.

"She didn't want to tell you. She said that you're trying really hard."

"Nice to know." I smiled to take the sting out of it, but it didn't help. I hated to think they were talking about me behind my back. I was such a perfectionist and hated proof to the contrary.

"Hey," I said, pivoting. "Do you have a lot of homework?"

"Nope. My teacher gave us time in class. We've got that concert tonight, remember?"

"Oh," I said, smoothing my expression. Sammie had called earlier in the week, asking if I could take Cookie to the holiday concert since Sammie couldn't wedge herself into the school's miniature theater seats with a bum leg. I'd said yes. Then promptly forgotten.

I'd never fully appreciated the mental load of raising a kid until I found myself tripping over it at every turn.

I snapped out of my distracted thoughts. "What time do we need to be there again?"

Maddie studied her mocha. My feeble attempt at a foam heart looked like a whole lot of nothing floating on the surface of her drink. "Um, I can get a ride with Jayden." She blurted it out, her voice a little too bright. "It's really no problem. He's going anyway," she mumbled, clearly expecting some pushback. "I have to be there early. This way, you can finish up whatever you're doing here and then swing by to get Cookie. She's really excited about going."

"I can manage both. No problem." Sammie had asked me to help out. I couldn't shirk my duties. My sister was stressed that her daughter had a little too much unchaperoned time. It had come up in one of our evening chats when she'd aired her suspicions that Maddie was holed up in her room, texting with Jayden. I had tried to be cool about my observations about the two, only confirming that the pair might be friendly.

Maddie sighed. "You don't have to run around. What if the roads are bad?" Outside the bakery, the roads appeared dry. And there was no forecast for snow. I had checked.

"Did you ask your mom if you could ride with Jayden? Who's driving?" Oh my goodness. Did he have a license? A whole lot of no-good could happen in a car.

"Mom told me to listen to you when I was here." Oh, good answer. I felt a smile tugging at the corners of my mouth. "And his uncle is driving us."

I dragged my lower lip through my teeth. She was one smart cookie. I didn't know anything about raising kids, but I did know what it was like to be a young girl. If I made a bigger deal of this than necessary, she'd be likely to go ahead and do whatever she wanted anyway.

Why are you making a big deal of this?

Probably because I remembered how Cookie had tried to monitor Sammie when she was hanging out with Trevor when they were teens. But kids were gonna do what kids were gonna do. And if you told a teen what they couldn't have, it made it more desirable.

My job was to keep the lines of communication open with my niece.

My heart expanded. Gosh, I loved this girl. "Okay, you can get a ride with Mr. Hemsley, but you'll go home with me and Cookie." Chaperones in place every step of the way.

Maddie's face lit up. "Deal." She went back to her mocha and pastry, chatting away about that evening's holiday concert.

"Hey, your mom said you've been brainstorming names for the bakery," I said after a while.

As she drank from the ceramic mug, Maddie's eyebrows crept up in silent surprise. She set the mug down and slid a small notebook out of the side of her backpack. Inside its pages were doodles—no, not exactly doodles—but rather complete artistic designs for the bakery signage. That girl had been hard at work.

She seemed to consider which ones to share. "How about Icing on the Cake? I thought it might tie in nicely with Top Shelf Brewery."

"Ah, you did?"

Maddie's face fell, and her cheeks grew red, making me regret my sarcastic comment. I quickly changed my tone. "I like it. What else do you have? Anything to play up the new coffee shop angle?"

She pursed her lips, flipping back and forth between pages. "I've got Rise and Grind, Wake and Bake Café, and Dough and Joe." We both giggled.

"Have you landed on a favorite?"

Maddie grimaced. "Not quite. I'll get there." She closed the notebook and stuffed it back into her bag. "Can I get ready in your apartment? I have my clothes here." She patted the side of her backpack.

I must have made a face because Maddie rolled her eyes. "Relax, it's my concert clothes. Everyone has to wear the same colors for the concert."

I held up my hands, pretending she hadn't read my mind. "I didn't say anything."

Maddie slung one strap over her shoulder. "You didn't have to." She gave me a look that was a hundred percent my sister.

I went in back and grabbed a few fresh loaves of bread that had been delivered this morning and filled the half-empty baskets out front. There was something very Zen about the slow pace of running a small-town shop. It was exactly the break I needed before I started my new stressful job in January.

**12 /
emily**

W hile Maddie was getting changed, I found myself lost in an Excel spreadsheet until a shadow came into my peripheral vision. Reflexively, I closed the lid of the laptop, ready to ask the customer how I could help them. Instead, I found Jayden shifting from one foot to the other, dressed in a crisp black suit and white shirt under a long, unbuttoned dress coat. He looked very handsome. Thick dark curls poked out from under a blue Buffalo Bills winter cap.

Technically, we hadn't met, so I smiled and said, "You must be Maddie's friend Jayden."

He jerked his head back, and one eyebrow drew down, as if he was surprised I knew his name. "Hi, yeah, I'm Jayden."

"Nice to meet you. I hear you're going to the concert together."

"Yeah." He casually stuffed his hands in his pockets and swayed.

"Okay, good. So Ted's driving?" I had no idea if Jayden could drive, but I felt the least I could do was confirm the transportation plans.

"Yeah. Do you know him?"

"Yes, we've met. He brought food during the storm last

week. It was very thoughtful of him." Unfortunately, the memory of those apple turnovers chose that moment to rear its undercooked golden head, and I promptly shoved my stupid embarrassment aside.

"That's Uncle Ted for you," he said, deadpan.

I casually gestured toward the back of the shop. "Maddie's getting changed. I'm sure she'll be down in a minute."

Jayden nodded. "Yeah, I texted her."

"Okay, cool." I held out my hand. "Want to sit?"

He shook his head. "I'm fine."

I ran the palm of my hand across the smooth edge of the table, searching my brain for small talk. I generally wasn't comfortable with silence. "Does the entire class have to participate in the holiday concert?"

Jayden shook his head. "Just those who take chorus. It's an easy A. And since I can squeeze it in mostly between football, basketball, and hockey, it works."

"You must be busy."

He hiked one shoulder and dragged his hand through the curly mop poking out from his hat. They called it the alpaca or broccoli cut. Saw it when I was scrolling online when I should have been doing something more important.

"It's not too bad," he said. "Most of my friends play at least two sports."

"Hi, Jayden." We both turned at the same time to see Maddie emerging from the back room. I stifled my initial response. *You look so grown up.* I didn't want to embarrass her.

Instead, I said, "You look nice." That didn't quite capture what I was thinking. My sweet niece who had a penchant for cozy sweatpants and chunky scrunchies was transformed by her fitted black skirt that fell below the knee and a frilly white blouse. In the short time that she had been up there, she had straightened her hair and applied pink lip gloss and mascara.

"Yeah, you look good," Jayden said, his voice cracking with emotion. The way he looked at Maddie—like she was the only thing in the world that mattered—made something tighten in my chest. I averted my gaze. Gosh, I remembered being a teen, feeling that heady rush of first love. And I knew all too well how it could lead to heartache.

"Okay, what time does the concert start?" I asked, probably too loud for the quiet space. "I should probably build in some buffer time to get Cookie there."

"It starts at seven," Maddie said with an edge that suggested I should have already known this. *Tough audience.* "The auditorium opens at six-thirty. Don't get there late because the seats fill up."

"Noted." I drew my lips into a thin line in response to being warned.

The sounds from out front grew louder, and I shifted to find Ted coming through the front door. He didn't have his silly hat on. He wore a dress coat and expensive-looking hiking boots that were both practical and stylish. "Hello, everyone." His eyes met mine, and I felt a warm flush flood my cheeks.

"Hello." I pushed my chair back and stood, instinctively folding my arms across my middle, but it wasn't the cold that made a shiver creep up my spine. Ted's steady gaze settled on me, and my stomach dipped just slightly, but enough that I had to remind myself to breathe. I cleared my throat and straightened my shoulders. "Thank you so much for taking Maddie."

"You're welcome." His brow lifted slightly as if he could sense my unease. "I'll make sure to deliver your niece safely."

"I have no doubt."

I was beginning to see how Cookie and Sammie had let things slide, despite the conflicts during the brewery's expansion. They had to find a way to live next door to these people, whereas from a distance, I could easily paint the Hemsley family as the enemy.

The bad guys.

But the man taking up too much space in the bakery, bundled in his winter coat, promising to deliver my niece safely to the school concert, didn't fit that role as neatly as I wanted him to. When it came to business in small towns and the families that ran them, there were obviously shades of gray.

"Got everything?" I turned to Maddie, who was buttoning up her coat. Jayden was holding her backpack and still wearing an absolutely smitten look on his handsome face. I cleared my throat, as if I had witnessed something I wasn't supposed to see. I wasn't sure why when it was all so sweet and innocent.

Maddie nodded.

"Cookie and I will be there at six-thirty."

"Don't be late," my niece said, tossing me another reminder. Had she no faith in me?

Jayden rushed ahead and held the door for Maddie. Ted lingered for a beat before giving me a big smile and repeating Maddie's warning. "Don't be late."

"It's not in my makeup." I flared my eyes wide, part flirting, part daring him to question me.

Ted's smile struck me like an arrow to the heart before he turned and followed the kids outside.

Maddie wasn't the only one in our family falling for one of the Hemsley men.

We walked a block down the street to where I'd finally managed to find a parking spot. One block. Not ideal, considering the wind was cutting through my coat. Man, winters could be brutal.

We really needed to figure out that parking mess. Thursday nights were big at the brewery because of Karaoke Night. People packed in like it was their last chance to belt out "Livin' on a Prayer." And that night, Galina had it handled.

Jayden climbed into the back of my extended cab truck, settling in next to Maddie. I stretched my arm across the back of the passenger seat, twisting to make sure he gave me his full attention.

"What am I? Your Uber?"

My nephew pressed his lips together, his expression eerily like his mother's when she got busted for breaking curfew back in high school. The look screamed, "Keep your mouth shut, dude."

I exhaled slowly, resisting the urge to smirk. I was still figuring out the line between being the *cool uncle* he could confide in and the *responsible guardian* who made sure he didn't do anything stupid.

Some days, it felt like a losing battle.

I stifled a laugh. I couldn't help it. The young man was more confident than I had been at that age by all accounts. I didn't come into my own until much later. Maybe if I had, I wouldn't have had my heart crushed.

Deciding to let it go, I turned around and pressed the ignition button. Embarrassing him further wouldn't gain me any points. And I suspected I was going to need as many points as I could get for far bigger issues. I'd been a teen boy once and could relate to the whole "trying to impress a girl" thing.

Still could. My mind went to Emily in the bakery, her long hair twirled in a tight bun at the nape of her neck. Her cheeks flushed, perhaps from baking. Gosh, if only she wasn't going to be leaving Walleye Point after Christmas. *Ah, the holidays.* That made me think of the boxes that had been delivered. They were clearly the decorations she had ordered for the bakery. Maybe I'd ask her to reconsider letting me put them up. Having the full block decked out would make both businesses look better.

The wipers skidded across the windshield, clearing the small dusting of snow. I pressed the button for the rear defroster. While giving the windows a moment to clear, I glanced into the rearview mirror. Maddie had her head tilted close to Jayden's, and she was saying something I couldn't hear.

Why hadn't I recognized this little crush sooner? Jayden and Maddie had been friends ever since my nephew came to live with my dad and Galina. Maddie had been a good friend, helping him transition to a new town, a new school. Before he moved here, the poor kid had gotten himself into a lot of trouble while trying to get attention from his mother.

A shadow crept over my mood at the thought of my bright, unstoppable sister whose fall into addiction had stripped away everything that should have mattered. I dipped my head and checked the side mirror for traffic before easing onto Main Street, trying to shake the familiar weight Amber's memory always brought. I couldn't change what had happened, but I could do right by the kid.

A car blared its horn, and I slammed on the brakes, immediately snapping out of my reverie. "Okay, buddy, I see you," I muttered.

"I'm going to remember that the next time you take me out driving," Jayden said from the back seat.

"Yeah, all right, easy, bud." I pulled out and headed toward the school. "How's the bakery going? Must have been tough after the disruption of the storm," I said, congratulating myself for making small talk that might just get me more information on her aunt without asking about her directly.

"Good, I guess," Maddie said. "It's never that busy anyway. My mom got some fancy coffee machines. I'm trying to figure out how to make latte art."

"Latte art," I said, trying to think if I'd had anything other than a coffee ground floating on the surface of my morning brew. "That's great."

"The Beanery has the best coffee," Jayden said, blissfully unaware that he'd failed at reading the room. He'd probably had their coffee once on a trip to Buffalo.

I shot him a warning look in the rearview mirror, but his focus was on Maddie.

"But they don't have Cookie's shortbread," I said, hoping to smooth over my nephew's not-so-subtle diss. "A full-on coffee shop would be a nice addition to Main Street, though."

Jayden mumbled something under his breath too quiet for me to catch. Maybe I was paranoid. Or maybe I just remembered what it was like to be almost sixteen and trapped in a vehicle with an adult making small talk while you were trying to impress a girl.

Not that my comment was dumb. But when you're his age, anything said by someone twice your age automatically registers as boneheaded.

"My mom is having my Aunt Emily go through the books," Maddie said. "Hopefully she can make the business more profitable."

My heartbeat stumbled at the mention of Emily.

Be chill, man.

I casually reached for the vent, pretending to adjust the airflow so I wouldn't miss a single word of what Maddie had to say next.

"Oh?" I asked, my tone as neutral as I could make it. "I heard she was only here until after the holidays?" I glanced into the rearview mirror and caught her frowning.

"That's what I heard."

"Hopefully they can make it work. It takes—"

Jayden groaned, cutting me off. "Uncle Ted."

I lifted my hands from the steering wheel in a gesture of surrender. "Just making conversation."

Maddie smiled in the rearview mirror. Maybe one of these kids was on my side. Apparently young ladies did mature before boys.

I held my tongue the rest of the drive and dropped the kids off at the bus loop. "See you in a little bit."

"Thank you for the ride, Mr. Hemsley," Maddie said as she scooted across the seat to exit on the same side as Jayden.

My nephew and Maddie headed toward the school entrance, Jayden shuffling ahead to open the door for his friend. A quick beep-beep from behind reminded me that I was holding up a line of traffic. I put the truck into gear and headed home to pick up Big Ed.

Driving home, I tried to remember if I had been clear enough in my birds-and-bees chat with Jayden. He and Maddie obviously had feelings for one another. Sure, I had spelled out the basics to eye rolls, grumbles, and "you've got to be kidding me." But was it enough?

Easy man, it's a well-chaperoned school event. He won't get in trouble.

Not tonight.

Unease washed over me. I slowed at the stop sign. Had I also emphasized the emotional aspects of dating and the subsequent entanglements? Had I stressed the importance of not breaking a young woman's heart? Especially when that heart belonged to the niece of a woman I'd love to get to know better.

Selfish much, man?

Another *toot-toot* had me check my rearview mirror. Shaking my head, I pulled through the intersection and drove the snowy streets toward home. I couldn't remember more snow being in the forecast. When I pulled up the driveway, Big Ed was standing in the doorway with his coat on already. I glanced at the dash. *6:15.* I didn't think the program at school started for another forty-five minutes. Gramps pushed open the door and locked it behind him, the screen door tapping him on the backside. He held the railing, taking each step tentatively.

I jumped out of the truck to meet him on the steps. "You're ready to go?"

"The good seats will be gone early."

"It's only a ten-minute drive," I said, wondering if this was a real thing or just his thing. My stomach growled. "I was hoping to get something to eat."

Gramps continued his descent of the steps, ignoring my comment. I held his elbow to steady him as we made our way to the car, giving up all hopes of grabbing something to eat.

We got back to Walleye Point High School in plenty of time to find seats a few rows from the stage. I wasn't sure I wanted to sit that close, but I made it a point not to argue with Big Ed. I glanced around the high school auditorium with its heavy curtains that had stood the test of time. Personally, I hadn't spent much time on that stage, save the occasional football or hockey awards ceremony where they even gave trophies to the bench warmers.

Lost in my thoughts, I watched Big Ed talk to a family who tried to scoot past us to the empty seats next to me. I leaned over. "I can move down."

Gramps waved his hand. "No, no." He stretched his hand past me. "Make sure you save those seats next to you."

"Why?"

I was mid-debate about whether I'd have the nerve to turn away another family eyeing the seats I was saving when I spotted Emily and her grandmother heading down the aisle. My breath hitched, just for a moment. Emily's hair hung loose around her shoulders, and the auditorium lights caught her eyes, bringing out the sharp blue. I cleared my throat and forced my gaze elsewhere before I got caught staring.

Ed leaned over and nudged me. "Those are open, right?"

Hadn't he just asked me to save them? That old coot. What is he up to?

"Sure, they're open." I rose to my feet, and Big Ed joined me.

"Scoot down two." Big Ed stepped out into the aisle to allow Emily and Cookie to take the seats between us.

"Nice to see you." I smiled, my gaze meeting Emily's. Her cheeks were flushed. I waited for her to sit before following suit. "Apparently, these are good seats." I wondered if my sarcasm was lost in the din of the gathering families.

"I suppose that depends on who you ask."

I might have been offended if I hadn't seen the twinkle in her eyes.

But probably not.

14 /
emily

Our *oh-so-innocent-looking* grandparents were definitely in cahoots. Cookie caught my eye and nudged my elbow before I could protest.

"Make sure you silence your phone."

I lifted my chin in agreement, dug into my purse, and shut off the ringer.

"I wish I had grabbed dinner first," I said to Ted, who furrowed his brow, clearly unable to hear me over the excited chatter of the crowd. My shoulder brushed against his as I repeated my comment.

Goodness. *How does one man generate so much heat?*

Ted turned his head slightly, his breath warm against my cheek. "You didn't eat either?"

That voice. Why did it have to be deep and rumbly? Totally unnecessary.

"Nope," I said then pressed my lips together. Professional. Composed. Not at all aware of how close he was.

"I thought I'd have time, too, but Big Ed ambushed me the second I got back from dropping off the kids."

I sighed. "Thanks for driving Maddie. I appreciate it." Even with that, I still hadn't found time to eat after closing the bakery and doing a quick check of my email. Still no updates from the job.

"No problem."

We locked eyes for the briefest of moments, and butterflies flitted in my stomach. *What am I doing?* I broke the stare and gestured vaguely at the flood of families pouring into the theater. "Apparently, this is the place to be." My tone was casual. Totally unbothered.

But my body felt twelve kinds of betrayed. My shoulder still tingled where it had brushed his, and the solid presence of his thigh, inches from mine, was setting off all kinds of fight-or-flight responses.

If I had been a turtle, I would have tucked my limbs inside my shell. Instead, I pressed my hands between my knees and strongly considered a strategic escape to the snack bar. I could return after the show started, at which point, I would be *forced* to find another seat.

"Apparently, it *is* the place to be," Ted murmured, echoing my statement.

I swallowed hard, the gruffness in his voice curling around me like a slow burn. I needed to pull it together. Channel my professional, take-no-garbage persona. The one that handled billion-dollar deals and did not get rattled by a competitor, a boardroom full of powerful men, or an impossible boss.

But being next to him was turning me into a mushy, lovesick sixteen-year-old.

And that was unacceptable.

I tried to swallow, but my throat was too dry. I never thought I was one to fall for a pretty face, but color me wrong. Ted was masculine, handsome, and so darned funny. A sense of humor was my weakness.

Ted placed his elbow on the arm of the chair between us. "Were you in the chorus in high school?" A rush of heat flooded my neck and cheeks as his arm brushed mine.

I casually plucked at the collar of my blouse and smiled. "No. I have no musical talents. What-so-*ever*."

"Me neither." He shifted in his seat, his knees whacking the seat in front of him. A woman with an inverted bob and a firm set to her mouth shot him an angry look over her shoulder. He held up his hand. "Sorry about that."

She spun back around with a huff.

Ted and I exchanged a quick glance, and I had to cover my mouth to stifle a laugh. Keeping my voice low, I said, "Let me guess, you were an athlete." I made a pensive face. "Mm, football. No, hockey. Hockey's the sport around here." The name of the brewery was Top Shelf.

He made a show of sitting up a little taller, catching himself when he almost bumped the back of the seat in front of him again. He widened his eyes as if to say, "That was close." Then he pressed his long fingers to his solid chest. "How could you tell?"

I felt a smile tugging at the corners of my mouth. "Which sport?"

"Both." An emotion I couldn't quite read flashed in the depths of his eyes. "But I preferred hockey."

"Why?"

Ted glanced down, rubbing his thumb over the thigh of his jeans like he was smoothing out some invisible crease. Half his mouth twisted into a grimace. "Football wasn't exactly my thing." His voice was light, but something flickered in his eyes, something heavy. "But my dad had other plans."

"Couldn't you tell him you didn't want to play?" I studied his profile as he stared at the empty stage.

"He was the football coach."

"Oh." My mind completely shut down at the display of vulnerability. The din around us seemed to dull, putting us in a little bubble of shared intimacy. "It must mean something that he chose a hockey-themed bar?"

He regarded me for a moment. The stage curtains fluttered open and the house lights dimmed, interrupting anything he might have said in response. On stage, the conductor tapped the top of the metal stand, silencing the audience.

Thankfully.

The concert started, and as much as I wanted to focus on the cheery holiday tunes, I couldn't. My attention was on the man sitting inches from me. He had me intrigued. Interested. But I wasn't staying in Walleye Point. So what was the point?

Nothing good could come from this. No matter how much Cookie and Big Ed conspired to put us together, it wasn't going to happen.

At intermission, I kept my hands clutched in my lap. Ted smiled over at me, a curious expression on his face. I feared the man could read my thoughts.

"The kids aren't bad."

I raised my eyebrows. "Oh, yeah, they were very good." I cupped my hand around my mouth and leaned closer so only he could hear. "I'm still starving, though."

Ted laughed. "Me too."

"There are snacks in the cafeteria."

"As much as I love Cookie's baked goods, I need something more substantial." Ted put his hand on his belly.

"Me too." My stomach growled at the thought. "I could go for a huge meatball from the Italian restaurant."

He dragged a hand across his jaw, the scratchy sound of his whiskers sending tingles down my spine. "Yes! And their Italian bread with pools of melted butter."

"I haven't had that in years." A headache formed behind my eyes, a sure sign I hadn't eaten enough today.

Cookie's giggle reached me, and I glanced over. She and Big Ed had their heads tucked close together in private conversation. Catching Ted's attention, I tipped my head toward our grandparents. "How long has this been going on?"

"A lifetime." Ted's steady gaze suggested it didn't surprise him.

It made sense. Big Ed ran the hole-in-the-wall bar on the same block as Cookie's bakery. Both had been widowed since before I could remember.

Maybe they had the right idea. They had an easy friendship that spanned decades. They were there for each other despite everything else going on around them. Maybe love wasn't about avoiding complications. Maybe it was about choosing to work through those differences, enjoying each other's company, and to heck with what anyone else thought.

A niggle of guilt prickled the hollow space in my chest. Why had I never discussed this with Cookie? Instead, we all seemed to treat her as our grandmother without an identity of her own.

Ted cupped the bend of the arm of the chair between us. I dug a fingernail into my thumb, trying to distract myself from my rioting nerves, unsure why this man had such an effect on me.

An announcement came over the PA, asking guests to return to their seats.

"I'm glad they have each other," I whispered close to Ted's ear, not sure what had gotten into me.

He turned quickly, perhaps surprised, too, and his whiskered jaw brushed my cheek. I jerked back, and a flush of warmth flooded my system. My stomach tightened in ways I wasn't prepared for. I snapped my attention to the stage, pretending kids filling the risers was the most fascinating thing ever.

On the other side of me, Cookie gently bumped my arm. "Hush, you two. Intermission is over." She made a show of acting stern, but I detected the glint of amusement in her eyes before the house lights dimmed.

Inwardly I shook my head. I couldn't wait to get out of

this stuffy room. A pool of sweat was gathering under my arms, and I was keenly aware of the space I took up.

"Have we been scolded?" Ted whispered, his breath tickling my neck. That did not help at all.

"We have," I whispered back, refusing to look at him.

"Too bad it's not for anything good."

Heat flooded my cheeks, and I had never been more grateful for the sound of sleigh bells as the chorus broke into a holiday favorite.

15 /

ted

Sitting next to me in the crowded auditorium, Emily gave off a familiar wound-too-tight vibe, like she was waiting to tell me she didn't belong here. Just like my ex had. My gut clenched. If I'd learned anything, it was that some people didn't stick around. Maybe it was Walleye Point.

Small town living wasn't for everyone.

Or maybe it was my situation. Not everyone could buy into raising someone else's kid. My ex certainly hadn't. Jayden needed a guardian—one who wasn't in his eighties— and the decision was easy for me.

Apparently, it had been easy for her too.

Better you find out now than later, random people would remind me when they stopped into the brewery and asked where she was. A downside of having a customer-facing job was that you had to face a lot of customers, and those people loved to give me their two cents about more than Top Shelf's featured beer.

My mind continued to wander as the high school chorus ran through a handful of holiday songs. When I tuned back in, two kids were performing a duet of "Baby, It's Cold Outside." Man, I was antsy. Not wanting to crowd Emily, I shifted a bit to my right, earning an under-the-breath "Take your half out of the middle, why don't you" from the stranger next to me.

They weren't wrong. I straightened.

"Sorry about that," I whispered.

Out of the corner of my eye, Emily remained still, engrossed in the concert.

When the last notes of yet another holiday favorite ended, the crowd erupted into applause. Cynical me wondered if it had more to do with the end of the concert—*finally*—versus cheering the talent. Maybe it was a little bit of both.

After the applause died down, I whispered to Emily, "Nice performance."

Big Ed sat at the end of our row, whispering in Cookie's ear. Her entire face lit up with laughter, making me wonder what comment had prompted such delight. Big Ed possessed a fantastic sense of humor and observed life with remarkable insight, though some of his observations weren't exactly suitable for young ears.

"It was," Emily said with all the warmth of the stranger on my other side.

She scooted forward and angled her body toward her grandmother, who made no attempt to move. "Where do we pick up the kids?" Her question was directed toward Cookie.

"In the cafeteria. Let's go." Cookie tapped Big Ed's thigh with the back of her hand.

He wrapped his work-worn hands around both arms of the chair and pushed himself up.

Emily slid to the edge of her seat with her back to me, her foot bouncing. Had I said something to offend her? I thought we had shared a few nice moments this evening, trapped in middle seats at the school concert.

Cookie reached behind her granddaughter and patted my arm. "They have light refreshments in the cafeteria. Will you join us? I know Big Ed was looking forward to having some of my shortbread."

Big Ed probably had a piece of Cookie's shortbread every day after lunch, even though he never seemed to go into the bakery, at least not through the front door. I made a conscious decision not to harass him. Simple pleasures were key after suffering the devastating loss of his only son.

"Of course," I said.

"The PTA has gone through a lot of work to set this up." Cookie slipped her hand around the crook of Big Ed's arm, and the two old friends joined the flow of family and friends making their way out of the auditorium.

Emily scooted out behind them, finding a small opening in the crowd. I followed, and without thinking, I placed my hand on the small of her back to prevent an eager parent from separating us. Emily glanced up and surprised me with a silly face, indicating the impatient woman who obviously couldn't see that everyone else was also trying to exit the auditorium. Emily's long hair brushed against my arm, sending an awareness coursing through my every nerve ending. If she didn't leave town soon, I was going to have to do something about these fleeting jolts of attraction.

If she'd let me.

The crowd jostled and bumped elbows as they snaked into the school cafeteria. Emily raced ahead of me to catch up to her grandmother. I scanned the crowd, hoping the kids would be dismissed soon so we could get out of here and get some real food.

"Why hello, Ted." One of the brewery's frequent patrons smiled up at me.

"Hi, Tina. Kids did a nice job, didn't they?"

Tina pressed one hand to her chest and the other to my arm. *Had she intentionally missed a few buttons on her shirt?* "I still can't believe I'm old enough to have a high schooler," she said. "Where does time go?" She seemed to be laying it on thick, her hand lingering on me. A few years ago, I might've flirted back just for fun. In that instance, it felt a little inappropriate.

I glanced around, hoping for my escape, but the gathering crowd only pushed us closer together. "It really does fly," I said without much emotion.

I nodded at whatever she was saying, figuring it didn't matter since we were exchanging inconsequential pleasantries. With all the jostling and chatter, it was hard to hear. After the third time I said, "What?" she pressed a hand on my chest once again and stretched up on her tiptoes.

"It's such a wonderful thing what you're doing with Jayden. I always…" Her words trailed off as Emily weaving through the crowd caught my eye.

I gently removed Tina's hand from my chest and pointed toward Emily. "I have to go."

Tina's eyes went wide, and before I could escape, she leaned in again, practically shouting in my ear. "Oh, is that your lady friend?"

As if Emily could sense we were talking about her, she turned just in time for our gazes to collide. Her lips twitched, not quite a smile, but not exactly indifference either.

"Have you met Emily?" I asked, relieved when a break in the crowd opened up a path to her. I placed my hand lightly against the small of Emily's back, feeling the warmth of her body through her sweater.

I leaned close to Emily's ear. "This is Tina."

Emily smiled tightly. "Nice to meet you."

"This is Cookie's granddaughter," I said. "She's helping out at the bakery."

Tina's eyes widened. "Oh, how is your sister? I heard about the accident."

"She's doing fine. Thanks." Emily ran a hand over her forehead.

"Well, I better go find my kids," Tina said.

"Goodnight," I said.

Emily let out an exaggerated breath and waved a hand in front of her face. "It's hot in here. I'm going to step into the hall." Her cheeks were flushed.

"Don't you want to get something to eat?" I kept my tone light, like her sudden shift hadn't lodged in my chest. "The baked goods look pretty decent."

Emily shook her head. "I need some air." Her smile wobbled. "Can you let Cookie and Maddie know I'll be in the hallway?"

"Yeah. Sure."

I watched her disappear into the corridor, one hand gripping the strap of her bag like it was anchoring her. A few minutes ago, we'd been crammed together in the world's smallest theater seats, her arm brushing mine every time she clapped, her laugh bubbling up at my commentary. We were having a good time... until Tina swooped in with her flirty grin and that too-loud "your lady friend" jab. Like maybe the town was keeping a list of them.

But Emily had gone quiet *before* that.

Which meant maybe it wasn't Tina. Maybe it was me.

Maybe I'd misread all of it—the teasing, the shoulder nudges, the way she hadn't moved away when our knees bumped. Maybe she thought I was the kind of guy who flirted with anyone who smiled at me. And since I worked at a bar, maybe I *was* a little guilty of that. I really needed to be more careful because the last thing I wanted to do was give Emily the wrong idea about me.

I scanned the cafeteria, the buzz of conversation suddenly grating. Cookie and Big Ed were still camped by the dessert table like someone had assigned them the task of guarding the goods.

I turned toward them, but my chest felt heavier with each step. Like I'd lost ground I didn't know I'd gained. Emily was the first woman in a long time that I'd actually wanted to get to know, and maybe this was the gut check I needed to remember why I'd stopped trying.

Walleye Point wasn't exactly the epicenter of high-paying jobs. My ex refused to move here when it became clear this was where I belonged. Maybe it was dumb to set myself up for heartache. Again.

16 /
emily

The cafeteria was sweltering, like someone had cranked the radiator just to mess with us. All the people chattering away in the tight space made my skin itch. My entire focus had turned to grabbing my family and going home.

And yet, there was Ted, leaning in close to some woman in the cafeteria, looking way too comfortable. I had no right to care. I'd just decided to tap the brakes after a bout of shameless flirting in the auditorium. Maybe it was the close quarters or the lack of food, but something had flipped a switch, reminding me how bad an idea this was. Ted probably thought I was a moody grump. But why should I care? I wasn't staying in Walleye Point. Starting something with him would only lead to a mess. For both of us.

I dragged my bottom lip through my teeth and scanned the room for Cookie and Maddie. I wanted to get out of here. Hunger was starting to gnaw at me, turning my annoyance into something hangry and sharp.

Finally, I spotted Cookie and Big Ed holding court near the dessert table. Naturally. I didn't have it in me to weave through the crowd with a smile pasted on. And worse? A stray disloyal thought snuck in, making me wonder if Big Ed was cozying up in hopes of nudging Cookie to sell the bakery to Ted.

Had working in the corporate world made me this cynical?

A kid came out of nowhere and hip-checked me. I bit back a complaint, which was herculean considering the mood I was in. I released a long, slow breath, trying to ignore how the colors of the crowd grew more defined, almost psychedelic. *Ugh.* I focused on the exit again, realizing I'd have to put on my big girl panties and breeze right past Ted and his companion.

After a quick introduction that was mostly swallowed up by a toddler who chose that moment to demand another cookie in what was clearly his outdoor voice, I asked Ted if he could round up Maddie and Cookie for me because I was ready to go.

Once he agreed, I made a beeline for the hallway. I held out my hand to separate two teens who seemed to be playing at a game of bumper cars, crashing into each other's shoulders then coming right back at it. Once I made it through the doors, I swore the temperature dropped twenty degrees, allowing me to catch my breath. I pressed myself against the wall, grateful for the cool tile and to be out of the way of pedestrian traffic.

Goodness, I really shouldn't go so long without eating.

Maddie burst out of the cafeteria, and her eyes brightened. Apparently, she had been looking for me. "Liam is having an after-party. Can I go?" She held out her arm behind her, and Jayden appeared, easing out of the crush of bodies, flapping the edges of his jacket as if that could cool him off. Apparently, I wasn't the only one who was hot.

"Oh, um…" I blinked a few times, feeling the heat gathering under my arms again. I cleared my throat to steady my voice. "It's a school night," I said automatically. A little voice in my head said, *Let her be a kid.*

Maddie clutched her phone like a lifeline. "Liam's parents are home. It's totally fine." I almost missed the subtle eye roll before she schooled her expression. I could be a pushover, but my niece knew better than to be disrespectful. "You can talk to my mom yourself."

"You asked your mom?"

"Yes, she said it was okay as long as you didn't mind taking us and picking us up." My niece turned on the full charm offensive, tilting her head and widening her eyes.

An uneasiness tightened in my gut. A lot could happen at parties. "Is this party going to be chaperoned?"

Maddie's shoulders sagged in exasperation. "Of course, Aunt Emily. I just told you that his parents will be there."

I pressed again. "And you're sure your mom's okay with this?"

"She likes Liam. Please, Aunt Emily."

"Sounds like fun." Ted rolled up behind his nephew, a ghost of a smile playing on his lips. *Not helping.*

I sighed. "Fine. But I need to take Cookie home first."

"Actually, Cookie says she's tired," Ted said. "Big Ed is going to drive her home in my truck. We have been tasked with getting the kids to the party." He must have registered something on my face because he added, "If that's not a problem."

"Of course it's not a problem. Let's go." I started to move toward the exit then glanced over my shoulder at Ted. "On second thought, I've got this. There's no sense both of us going when you can make sure our grandparents get home safely."

That slow, easy smile brightened his face. "You're not going to ruin this for them, are you?" I couldn't be sure whether he was talking about Maddie and Jayden or Cookie and Big Ed.

"I'm not a buzzkill," I muttered, my mood moderately lifting because I was minutes away from getting out of here.

He lifted an eyebrow, amused. "That's exactly what a buzzkill would say."

I guess he's going with us.

I turned to Maddie. "Ready?" A trickle of sweat rolled down my back. "Go tell your grandma we're leaving."

"Already done," Ted said.

"Aren't you helpful."

"I aim to please." He held out his hand, his gaze lingering just a little too long. "Now, where are you parked?"

I hesitated then ignored the blaring warning signs that this was a bad idea. "This way."

emily

Maddie and Jayden bolted back into the school, one of them apparently having forgotten something they absolutely couldn't get tomorrow. I didn't bother asking what. It seemed this night was going to play out however it wanted, with or without my approval. Why fight fate?

I didn't bother to button my coat as I carefully navigated the ice rink posing as a parking lot. "You know, I could've dropped the kids off myself. You could've gone home with Big Ed and Cookie."

Ted fell into step beside me, hands shoved into his coat pockets. "You're really trying to get rid of me, aren't you?" When I didn't reply, he said, "Liam's family lives out on Rusty Creek Road. It's tricky to find."

A part of me bristled at the idea that I needed some big, strong man to protect me from the treacherous wilds of Walleye Point. The other part—the part that knew how much I loathed driving down pitch-dark, icy country roads with deer looking to ruin my night—reluctantly agreed.

Still. Years of climbing the corporate ladder in a male-dominated industry had left me with an instinctive, knee-jerk reaction to anyone, even a well-meaning, handsome someone, implying I needed help. I imagined flexing my muscles, beating my chest, and announcing "Me, independent woman!"

Instead, I muttered, "I would've been fine." Deep down, I knew my reluctance to spend more time with Ted came from something altogether different.

I reached into my purse, blindly fumbling for my key fob while keeping an eye on the school doors. The kids reemerged, and I waved to let them know where we were.

"Are you comfortable with Big Ed driving?" I asked, shifting gears to something that mattered. I might not love driving in the dark, but Cookie's safety trumped my ego.

Ted shot me a look. "My grandfather's a good driver."

"I'm a good driver too." The words tumbled out before I could stop them. I immediately cringed. Oh great. I sounded like a five-year-old demanding a gold star.

Ted's lips twitched, like he was fighting a smile. "Never said you weren't."

I huffed out a breath, pressing the key fob until my vehicle's lights flashed. I needed to stop being so defensive. I sighed, momentarily nostalgic for my old life where the only person I had to worry about was myself.

When we reached the car, Ted said, "I'd ask if you wanted me to drive…" The statement lingered out there.

He wanted to drive my car. My baby? "I don't share well," I said.

"Duly noted." He opened the passenger door and climbed in.

I took a deep breath before slipping behind the wheel and starting the ignition, adjusting the controls to clear the windows.

The muffled laughter of the kids reached me before they did. I clicked the locks. In the side-view mirror, Jayden opened the back door for Maddie, then he jogged around and climbed in the other side.

The young couple giggled and chatted in hushed tones. A whisper of nostalgia for the innocence of youth washed over me. I had been so serious, even as a teen. I didn't mess much with boys, probably because I was studying all the time. However, there had been one *almost* boyfriend that summer. The last summer I was forced to stay with Cookie in Walleye Point.

Before everything changed.

I adjusted the heat and control settings while Ted and I sat without speaking, waiting for the front windshield to defrost. I was still so darn hungry. The silence hung over us like some awkward passenger until I finally came up with some small talk. "I like to make sure the window has a big clear spot before I drive."

"No problem."

"Thanks for driving us," Jayden said from the back seat. "Do you know how to get there?" The sound of seat belts snapping in place punctuated the question.

"Out on Rusty Creek. Your friend that hosted the football party," Ted said.

"Yeah, that's it," Jayden said.

In the rearview mirror I saw Maddie refreshing her lip gloss. I hesitated, wondering if this was something I should worry about.

Easy, it's lip gloss.

I reached for the GPS display. "Want to give me the address?"

Ted held up his hand. "No need. I'll navigate."

I let out a quiet sigh. I preferred to see where I was going for myself.

"I won't leave you hanging," Ted said, obviously reading my mood.

I cut him a sideways glance, not convinced. I put the car into gear and made my way out of the parking lot while Ted gave me clear and concise directions, allowing plenty of advance warning for turns, although I was loath to admit it.

We made our way down Main Street. A few cars lingered in front of the brewery. Apparently, Ted wasn't kidding. The diehards had shown up for karaoke night even in this weather. A block away, the white Christmas lights on a gazebo cast the town square in a warm halo. Very Hallmark vibe-y.

"That looks really pretty." For a moment, I wasn't in my expensive car with a man who made me question everything. I was sixteen again, flush with the heat of puppy love, running across the square in my new Converse like I was one of the in crowd, having caught the attention of that cute townie who made it easy for me to pretend I was something I wasn't.

"Have you ever spent a winter in Walleye Point?" Ted asked.

"A couple times we'd drive in to visit my grandma around the holidays. We'd celebrate with Cookie once the rush at the bakery was over." But mostly it was the long, lazy summers that I was forced to fritter away in this sleepy town. It allowed my mom to work full-time in Buffalo while Cookie provided free babysitting. It wasn't that my grandmother had idle time; it was more that she allowed children in her place of work, while Mom's didn't.

I glanced up in the rearview mirror and caught Jayden playfully poking the sleeve of Maddie's puffy jacket.

My niece suddenly sat straighter and pointed out the window. "Look, the ice rink is up. My mom said you guys skated on it one Christmas."

I laughed. "Oh gosh, I'd forgotten. We had to rent skates, and we both ended up with blisters. I'd love to do that again." I wasn't sure why I was feeling wistful.

Jayden piped up. "The rink at The Point Center is better maintained."

I caught Ted's gaze briefly before I turned my attention back to the road in front of me. I guessed today's teens were more particular. I looked both ways and proceeded through the intersection. "The Point Center? Sounds fancy."

"It replaced the old community center. Hockey has exploded in popularity in the past decade or so, even more than when I played," Ted said.

"I'm having my birth—" Jayden cleared his throat and lowered his voice. "I mean, I'm having a few kids over to the rink next Saturday for my birthday. Maybe you can come. Hang out. And stuff."

"Yeah, maybe," Maddie said, clearly pleased. "Snap me the details."

When I glanced in the rearview mirror again, Jayden was huddled over his phone, tapping away with two thumbs. I'd have to update Sammie on the situation.

"Turn here," Ted said, startling me. I'd almost forgotten he was my personal navigation system.

I made the turn as instructed and found myself gripping the steering wheel as my high beams swept into the snowy landscape all around me.

Maddie placed her hand on the back of my seat. "It's up here."

I slowed and pulled over behind a minivan dumping a bunch of kids out at the end of a long driveway.

I was about to ask what time they needed to be picked up when Jayden said, "Liam's mom says we need to be picked up in an hour."

An hour? It hardly seemed worth the drive home and back. I sighed. "Fine. I'll be back in sixty minutes."

"You should go check out the Christmas lights in the square," Maddie said oh-so-casually. "Easier than driving back and forth."

I suddenly became aware of my heart beating in my ears. Was she matchmaking?

Before I could respond, both kids bailed, joining a pack of friends as they strode toward the glowing house.

I squinted as Jayden and Maddie passed under the porch light. Something about the way they walked side by side made my stomach do a weird flip. I glanced at Ted.

"Were they holding hands?" My voice shot up an octave.

Ted tipped his head, his smirk full of barely contained amusement. "Looks that way. Apparently, my nephew's got game."

I narrowed my eyes. "Well, your little Romeo better keep his hands to himself." I put the car in drive and pulled away from the house. "Now, TedNav, lead me back to town. We have to find food."

Ted chuckled, low and warm. "Jayden is a good kid. They'll be all right." He shifted in his seat. "And why do you just assume he's a Romeo?"

"Directions please," I said, ignoring his question.

"Why do I think this has more to do with me than my nephew?" His tone was teasing, but something in his choice of words made my heart race.

I exhaled through my nose. "Does this personal navigation system come with a mute button?"

Ted grinned. "How will you find your way if I go silent?"

"I'll manage." I did a three-point turn, flicking my blinker on. "This way?"

"Yes, ma'am."

18 /
ted

O nce we reached town, I turned to Emily. "I have a surprise."

She cut me a sideways glance. "Should I be concerned?"

"I promise you'll like it."

Earlier, she'd mentioned how much she was craving meatballs from the Italian restaurant in town. So I called in a favor. Even though the kitchen had closed ten minutes ago, a friend had left two meatball subs waiting at the hostess stand. The place was dark, the staff inside counting the drawer and finishing up the dishes, but that glorious smell hit me the second I ran in to grab it.

When I returned to the car, Emily hugged the bag to her chest. "You are officially my favorite person right now."

"Good to know. I'll try not to let it go to my head."

We parked near the gazebo and dug into the food. Neither of us said much, too busy inhaling meatballs and melted cheese to bother with conversation.

When the last bite disappeared, I wiped my hands on a napkin and leaned back with a satisfied sigh. "We could use dessert."

Emily's eyes narrowed, her hand frozen mid-swipe at

marinara in the corner of her mouth. "Did you ever try those apple turnovers I made?" There was something cautious in her tone.

I nodded. "I did. They were…" I paused, only slightly, for dramatic effect. "Memorable."

She groaned and chucked her balled-up napkin at my chest. "You're a terrible liar. Maddie already spilled the beans. She said the apples were too hard."

I shrugged, unfazed. "I wasn't about to complain. Free pastries are free pastries."

"Even the bad ones?"

"Builds character."

Her laughter came easily. "Just for the record, I got distracted while baking. I'll master them next time."

"I can't wait. Come on. Let's take a walk and work off these subs." I gathered up the garbage and stuffed it into the bag. "We can admire the lights too."

She made a vague sound of agreement. "I suppose. I can't remember the last time I really slowed down to admire Christmas lights. Anywhere."

"You were eyeing the ones at the brewery."

Emily let out a soft snort. "Did you ever finish putting those up?"

The teasing note in her voice made it clear she wasn't impressed, but the truth was, the brewery looked great. It was the bakery next door that looked like it had given up on the holidays altogether.

I shot her a knowing look. "Oh, just you wait."

She had no idea I'd recruited Big Ed to grab the decorations she'd ordered. With Cookie's blessing, I had a plan to surprise her with the finished product.

"The town gets quiet at night. And goodness, it's peaceful." Some of the tension she'd carried like armor since the concert finally eased from her shoulders. Whatever had gotten under her skin seemed to drift off into the cold night air, but not completely.

It still seemed to hover just below the surface, waiting to reemerge if I said the wrong thing. So I chose not to address it.

"Yeah, it is quiet."

The park was empty, silent in that magical small-town way. Main Street had gone mostly still, the lights in the shop windows flicked off one by one. I used to pass the town center on Christmas Eve after church and think the lights would act as a beacon for Santa and his sleigh. That wasn't the only magical memory tied to this place.

"All the smart people are probably home on the couch watching Netflix," she said with a quiet laugh.

"Except the ones with kids."

My thoughts drifted to Galina, my father's widow. Most nights after her shift, she holed up in her room with the TV on low, trying to live a life she never signed up for. But she showed up and did her best, and I tried to do right by Jayden in return.

I reached for the car door, and the dome light popped on, allowing me to catch a faraway look in Emily's eyes. I wondered if a memory from her past in this place had caught her unaware. Made her feel as nostalgic as it made me feel. "Come on," I said gently. "Let's stretch our legs."

"Okay." She climbed out, clutching the collar of her coat.

I met her around the front of the car and kept my arm near her elbow in case she lost her footing. Those boots didn't look like they had much traction. We found the walking path that cut through the square, but it had a few inches of snow. The town did a good job of clearing the path with these little four-wheelers with a plow in front. But they weren't miracle workers against the falling snow.

Emily sighed and flipped up her hood but not before a gust of wind sent a strand of hair brushing across her cheek. I resisted the urge to brush it away. What was it about this woman that had me noticing things? Her hair, her cynical look, the way she held the edge of her hood like she wasn't sure this was a good idea.

"Want to go back? The wind is pretty wicked."

"Let's walk a little farther." She quickened her pace. The snow squeaked under her dress boots. "I really needed this. I'm sorry if I was rude earlier."

"No worries. Nothing a meatball sub won't cure," I said, deflecting. I had a hunch her mood wasn't just about hunger, but I appreciated the apology.

We went a few feet, then Emily muttered something under her breath. She turned toward me. "I forgot to video the concert for Sammie." She slanted a glance at me accusingly, like I had something to do with it. "Darn it."

Ah, maybe I had distracted her. I liked to think that I had that kind of power, but of course, I didn't. She was just beating herself up for forgetting.

"I'm sure you could put a shout-out on some social media platform, and ten parents would offer you theirs. You could do a video compilation from every angle," I said, strolling toward the center of the park. A soft gust of wind lifted a dusting of snow. The twinkling lights made the flakes look like glitter in a snow globe.

That video comment earned me a smile that warmed my heart. I liked making Emily smile. I remembered we had done a lot of laughing that day all those years ago.

Right back here.

"I feel bad Sammie had to miss the concert, but it's good that she's taking it easy." Emily walked slowly until we reached the gazebo. "She needs to be back at it right after the holidays. I can't stay a day longer."

"You strike me as the type of person who doesn't like to have her plans altered."

Still clutching her hood, she turned her back to the wind. The lights lining the gazebo allowed me to catch the pinched expression on her face suggesting she didn't take that as a compliment. I much preferred her smile.

"No offense meant. You just strike me as very organized."

"I am, almost to a fault." Emily's gaze grew dreamy. "I need to learn to live in the moment."

"Not a bad quality," I said, relishing every detail of *this* particular moment.

"My job requires me to always be thinking three steps ahead."

"Cookie mentioned you're a bank teller." I held my breath, waiting for her response, knowing full well a bank teller's wages couldn't support the bakery.

The white lights danced in her eyes, and I sensed she knew I was playing with her. "Is that what Cookie said?"

With my hands stuffed in my pockets, I shrugged. "You're not a bank teller?" Sure, Cookie mentioned Emily worked in banking, and some people might automatically think of a bank teller, at least a lot of the people I knew. They had no exposure to finance, nor could I claim to be much of an expert either.

She turned to meet my gaze. "I work in finance."

"So, you're not a bank teller?" I didn't bother to hide my smile.

She rolled her eyes and shuddered when another gust of wind whipped up.

I peeled off my hat and immediately missed its warmth. "Here." I extended the cap to her. It wasn't as warm as the one I wore while doing work around the brewery, but it was better than nothing.

Emily shook her head.

"Come on." I stepped closer. "You won't slug me if I put my hat on your head, will you?"

She sighed heavily, as if exasperated by me, then shook her head. I gently put it on her, careful to tug it down over her ears. I pulled off one of my gloves and swept the hair out of her eyes. "Oops, sorry about that." I cocked an eyebrow. "It does look great."

She tugged the knit fabric lower on her head. "It feels pretty great too." She wiggled her nose and blinked rapidly, as if forcing the last bit of hair out of her eyes. "I would have packed more gear if I'd realized I was going to go out in the elements." She reached out, and her hand hovered over me, a look of amusement brightening her eyes. "Steam is coming off your head."

I was going to make a deadpan joke about being hot but decided to keep it to myself. I wasn't convinced she'd appreciate it, even though she had teed me up for a perfect shot.

When Emily's focus shifted to a bunch of laughing kids running down the sidewalk on the edge of the park, I took the opportunity to study her profile. Her perfect nose, her high cheekbones, and her long lashes. I would have loved to know what she was thinking. Did she remember standing in this gazebo that summer?

Another whoop rose from the teenagers who had spilled out of the ice cream shop, their laughter echoing across the street.

"The time-honored tradition of grabbing ice cream after a school event," I said. "Back when life felt a whole lot simpler."

She let out a soft sound somewhere between a laugh and a scoff. "I was raised by a single mom. We didn't go out for ice cream much." Her tone wasn't bitter, just honest. "Don't get me wrong, my mom did right by us. We had every opportunity. More than she ever did."

She stopped there, but I had the sense that she'd edited the end of that sentence, perhaps something about this town and what it hadn't given her mother.

"Where is your mom now?"

Emily laughed. "Working. Turns out she has a big job with a bank in Buffalo." She playfully wagged her finger at me.

"And she's not a teller either. Not that there's anything wrong with that. But somehow people always assign women the jobs of tellers and men every other job in banking or finance."

She was right. "Sorry, guess I should get…" I was about to make a joke then decided to claw it back. She deserved more. "Cookie actually confessed that she wasn't sure exactly what you did, but she said she was impressed. That you had an important job in finance." I paused a beat. "Impressive."

She crossed her arms over her coat and bounced on the balls of her feet. "I worked hard to get where I am. It's fortunate that I'm between jobs right now, affording me the time to give Sammie a hand at the bakery."

"I'm sure your sister appreciates your help. And Cookie."

"I do what I can." She took a step back and rested against the railing of the gazebo. "What about your work? Do you like working at the brewery?"

"I do." I really did. "My dad had the dream of turning Big Ed's old hole-in-the-wall into a newfangled brewery." That was what my grandfather called it. "Once he realized others were investing in Walleye Point, he decided to take the plunge." I ran my hand across the back of my neck. "I wasn't part of that process."

Emily's brow furrowed.

"He was a few months out from opening when he had a heart attack. His wife, Galina, begged me to help get the place open. Until he got back on his feet." I cleared my throat. "We thought he was getting better," I said, my throat tight. "He was barking out orders from the ICU like he'd be back at the brewery in no time." I released a slow breath. "He should have listened."

The words sat between us, heavy with everything I hadn't said. I missed my dad. I wasn't sure I'd ever lived up to his vision. Maybe I was never meant to run a brewery, but here I was.

Emily took a step closer and touched my arm. "I'm so sorry."

Emotion choked me, making it hard to speak. I swallowed, letting a beat pass before forcing out "I'm sorry too."

I hesitated, my breath clouding the cold night air. "My dad was a bulldog. Stubborn as all get out. But he had a vision for the brewery, a real plan. He would have loved seeing it thrive." I exhaled, a bittersweet smile tugging at my lips. "I like to think I'm doing him proud."

Emily's expression was unreadable. "The business is booming." Her voice was even, measured. "And I love that he made it hockey-themed, considering football was his thing."

That made me pause. A thick layer of snow coated the gazebo benches. It wasn't the first time I'd considered that maybe his hockey-themed brewery had been his way of trying to connect with me, the son who had failed to love football the way he did. The son who loved hockey.

I huffed out a soft laugh and turned back to Emily. "I'm sorry if all the extra customers are taking up your parking spaces." I flashed a half smile, falling back on humor like a well-worn defense mechanism.

A small smile curved her lips. "It has definitely been a challenge. But I can see Cookie and Big Ed haven't allowed it to impact their friendship."

"The old guard," I said. That's how I often thought of them. They valued relationships. We could learn something from them.

"If the bakery closed tomorrow, Cookie should be fine. She has enough money to do what she wants, including fixing up her little cottage in town." Emily worried her bottom lip, as if she was about to say something but then decided to hold it back.

"Big Ed has been helping with the renovations," I said.

"Really? I thought she had a contractor?"

"Who is an old buddy of my grandfather's. He's advising and even rolling up his sleeves."

"Neither seems to know how to retire."

I flipped up my collar against the cold. "Keeps them young, I guess."

"Yeah, they're lucky to have one another." She turned away to stare over the snowy park. "Do they still have the carnival here in the summer?"

"They do." The wind might've been biting, but suddenly I was warm all over.

She turned back to face me, her eyes softer now, clouded with something that looked a lot like recognition. A memory, maybe. Something old and half-buried rising to the surface.

I wanted to believe she remembered.

But maybe that was just me, clinging to a flicker of hope I had no business holding onto.

19 /
emily

Something in Ted's gaze shifted, like he was looking right through me. The spark in his brown eyes sent me tumbling back. Not to this snowy night in the park, but to a summer afternoon drenched in sunshine. The scent of funnel cakes, the blur of the Tilt-A-Whirl, green grass, flip-flops, and the freedom of being sixteen.

How had I not seen it before?

Heat surged beneath my coat, blooming across my chest like a secret finally remembered. A ribbon of nostalgia curled up my spine, tightening my throat.

"The carnival," I said, my voice lighter than I felt, "was one of the only things I actually liked about summers here. Cookie would hand us a twenty and tell us to make it last all day." I gave a half laugh, the memory oddly vivid now. "We thought we were so independent. Even if we were technically still in spitting distance of the bakery. We never got to do stuff like that back home."

The words spilled out. Maybe I didn't want to stop. Maybe admitting it out loud helped me believe what I already knew deep down.

"For that week, we got to pretend we belonged. That we

were townies. Sammie and I were always the outsiders, watching from the edges, hoping we blended in just enough." I glanced toward the gazebo, its lights dusting the snow with a soft golden glow. "I didn't mind being anonymous. Back then, I could be anyone I wanted. Not the smart girl hustling babysitting jobs to save for college. Not the overachiever." I looked back at him. "I was the mysterious summer girl. Whatever version of me I wanted to be."

His eyes didn't leave mine. And suddenly, I wasn't so sure I was the only one who remembered.

"I like to think us townies were a welcoming bunch." Something in the twitch of his mouth sent a shiver down my spine. Like déjà vu, but more distinct. Familiar. No? That wasn't possible.

"Did you spend a lot of time at the carnival?" I asked, narrowing my eyes.

He gave a single nod, never breaking my gaze.

"That was a long time ago. We were just kids," I finally said, unable to deny it anymore.

"I remember it like it was yesterday," he said, reaching out and taking my hand.

I couldn't find the words as another memory slammed into me. A baby-faced sixteen-year-old with bleach-blond hair. "You had blond hair."

"The football team made us dye it. School spirit and all." The way he searched my face made my whole body vibrate. "You were a smart, sassy city girl. I couldn't believe my luck when you agreed to hang out with me at the carnival."

"Oh?" My voice squeaked, and I was feeling very much like that sixteen-year-old girl, reveling in that week of freedom. Of reinvention. Of being someone else. But now, standing here with him, I didn't want to be someone else. I just wanted to be me.

"It took you a long time to remember," he said, his voice

quieter now. He gave a short laugh, shaking his head. "You certainly know how to humble a guy."

A flicker of guilt flared in me. The memory was so vivid now. The way he flipped his head to get his hair out of his eyes. The firework-lit sky. The way I had felt that night. But how? I never knew a Ted. Like, probably ever. It wasn't common among boys I'd known—not like Alex or Tyler or Zander.

"You didn't go by Ted back then." The world seemed to tilt and still all at once, like we'd stepped out of time. "Eddie," I said, my voice catching on the memory. I smiled, remembering how cute I'd thought the name was. "I can't believe you didn't tell me."

He gave a half shrug, something self-conscious in the movement. "I got tired of being Little Eddie. Switched to Ted in college."

My thoughts spun. I scratched at the back of my head, the knit cap suddenly itchy. "How did you recognize me? I'd like to think I'm a little less awkward than that scrawny teenager."

"I didn't, not right away," he said, reaching up to adjust the rim of my hat. His fingers grazed my cheek, sending sparks straight to my spine. "But once I found out you were Sammie's sister, it clicked. Cookie has photos of you guys hanging in the bakery. I made that connection a few weeks later when I stopped in to grab donuts." He released a quick breath through his nose. "Imagine my surprise."

We had never exchanged last names. And while I was trying to put all the pieces together, he said, "And you used to hang out with my sister, Amber."

"Amber?" I blinked. "The barefoot girl with the wild hair? Sammie adored her. They were inseparable that summer." The words came out soft. "Amber was such a free spirit."

His expression shifted to something more somber. "That's her. That's Jayden's mom."

The breath caught in my throat. "Oh." A beat passed. "I'm so sorry."

He nodded, clearing his throat. "Yeah. I miss her. I still hope she finds her way back."

I reached for his hand again without thinking, lacing our fingers for a moment before letting go and pressing my palm to my face. "This feels like a lifetime ago."

He didn't disagree.

"I can't believe you didn't say anything sooner." I shook my head, thinking back through everything I'd said and done since I arrived back in Walleye Point. "Goodness, have I been ridiculous?"

"No," he said gently. "You've been real. I like real."

But my heart still pinched. "We were supposed to meet the next morning at the dock for a goodbye."

His eyes held mine, steady and warm. "Yeah," he said, not unkind. "But you didn't show."

I opened my mouth to apologize again, but he stopped me with a soft shake of his head and a tilt of his chin toward the lawn. "That night, we stood right over there. Under the tree, behind the waffle stand."

And just like that, the whole memory came rushing back, as vivid as those fireworks in the sky.

I let out a long breath and dipped my head. "I remember." I wondered if he had the same memories. Bits and pieces that sprang to mind, blended with other firsts like my apartment or job or living away from home.

I bit my lower lip.

With my eyes firmly closed, I recalled how sixteen-year-old Ted had taken my hand and pulled me under the tree. Everyone else's attention was on the fireworks, celebrating the last night of the carnival. A million scenes from the romance novels I'd read voraciously as a kid played out in my head. My entire body was on fire. It was overwhelming.

Just like in my novels, he closed the distance between us,

pressing my back against the bark of the oak tree. It wasn't as big then. He did that hair flip thing, and I could barely think straight. He cupped my cheek with a hand calloused from stick handling in hockey.

I opened my eyes to find Ted watching me intently. He took a step closer, his hand grazing my cheek, the heat of it grounding me in a way that sent my heart into overdrive. Was he remembering what I was remembering? How he dipped his head and pressed his warm lips on mine.

Over a lifetime ago.

I could still see sixteen-year-old Ted. Bleach-blond hair. That easy smile. The boy I had kissed, probably with chapped lips and popcorn breath. Then I'd made the mistake of checking the phone that had buzzed in my pocket. It was Sammie, telling me we had to go—*now*. Something about the timing of the text made me feel like I had done something wrong. That it had been about me and Ted.

"I handled things wrong," I whispered, completely distracted by his touch. "I suppose I thought it was stupid to have feelings for you when I was going back to Buffalo the next day."

"So you did have feelings for me." His mouth curved into a teasing smile, but his eyes told a different story—soft, searching, and more than a little hopeful.

"You really are insufferable." I swatted at him playfully, and he caught my bare hand in his.

"I often thought if I had had a do-over with that kiss, that you would have shown up on the dock the next day." Earlier that day we had vowed to meet at the dock at sunrise before I went home.

"Oh yeah?"

"Yeah." He dropped his hand from my cheek and held it out. "Here's your chance to escape."

I shook my head. "I'm not a little girl anymore." Oh gosh, where did that come from? Something about this man.

He leaned in, slow enough for me to stop him if I wanted. I didn't want to.

His lips brushed mine, just a whisper of warmth against the cold, and everything in me tightened and unraveled at the same time.

**20 /
ted**

Emily's lips were softer than I remembered, warm despite the chill in the air. I wrapped my arm around her, pulling her closer, deepening the kiss, and savoring the quiet, breathy sound she made in response. Then a gust of wind barreled through, sharp and relentless, slamming us back into the moment.

We broke apart, laughter bubbling up between us as we ducked our heads, our foreheads pressing together like we could block out the cold and maybe the fact that we'd just crossed a line we couldn't uncross.

I reached up, adjusting her hood to shield her from the wind. "I've been waiting a very long time to do that again."

She squinted up at me, a suppressed giggle on her face. "I'm not a fan of PDA."

I glanced around. "Good thing we're alone then."

She shook her head. "Why didn't you tell me who you were that first day I parked in front of the brewery?"

I grinned, dragging a knuckle along the curve of her cheek. "Honestly? I was only ninety-nine percent sure it was you."

"That's all, huh?"

"I didn't want to make a fool of myself. And then I

wanted to see how long it would take before you figured it out."

She reached up to rake her fingers through her hair, only to be met with my hat still snug on her head. "That doesn't seem fair. I can't imagine how I came off. I was stressed from driving in the storm." With a sigh, she pulled it off and held it out to me. "How embarrassing."

My brow furrowed. "I didn't mean to embarrass you."

Her lips parted slightly, her breath coming out in a cloud of vapor between us. "I guess I've been so wrapped up in my own problems, I didn't see what was right in front of me."

I leaned in, brushing my lips over hers again, this time softer, slower, like I was giving her time to catch up. When I pulled back, I held her gaze. "If I'd told you sooner, would we have gotten here sooner?"

Her cheeks were bright pink, but I suspected that had more to do with the weather than embarrassment or anything else. "I guess we'll never know."

"I went to the dock the next morning," I said, finally risking brutal honesty while I settled the hat back on her head.

Her eyes grew red-rimmed, and she pressed her hand to her lips. "I wanted to meet you. To say goodbye."

"Then why didn't you?" I searched her face for the answer, not sure why it mattered all these years later. Everything seemed to matter so much more in those teenage years.

She dropped her hand away from her face. "You know how sad it makes me feel to think of you waiting there alone for me?"

"I was bummed for sure."

"So much happened that night. I couldn't leave the house." She tugged on one side of the hat. "I wished you had texted me. I could have explained."

"Remember I entered my phone number in your phone?" I asked. "I didn't have your number."

Emily took a step back and bumped into the railing. She reached back to brace her hands on it then, probably realizing it was frozen, clasped them in front of her. "You remember all that?"

"Some things stick." We stared into each other's eyes for a long moment before I held out my hand and took hers. "Come on. Let's get in the car before we freeze to death."

We ran-walked back to the car and climbed in. We still had twenty minutes to kill before we had to pick up the kids from the party.

Behind the wheel, she started the car and cranked up the heat. Rubbing her hands together, she finally spoke. "You should have told me who you were right away."

"Why?"

She shrugged, like she didn't have an answer. Or maybe like she had too many.

I knew mine. I wanted to get to know her without the weight of our past tilting the scales. Without her seeing me through the lens of that teenage summer and old heartbreak. When she didn't show up the next morning, it stung. More than it should have. It took me right back to every time my dad had torn into me on the football field, reminding me I'd never measure up. Not to him. Not to his expectations. Never mind that I didn't even like football. I only wanted to play hockey.

I glanced at her, waiting.

Emily didn't say anything at first, just kept staring through the windshield like the lights in the park held all the answers she wasn't ready to face.

I studied her profile in the glow from the gazebo. Her strong jaw, those lashes brushing high cheekbones, and that stubborn tilt of her chin that told me she was already pulling away. Retreat mode. I'd seen it before. Man, I'd lived it the morning she didn't show up at the dock.

"I'm not trying to tie you down," I said quietly. "I just

don't want to let go before we've even figured out what this is."

Her hands tightened on the wheel like she was bracing for impact. "You make it sound easy."

"It's not." I ran my thumb across my lower lip. "But it's worth it."

She finally turned to me, her expression unreadable. "I don't know how to do casual."

My heart thudded. "Then don't. Let's just be real. No timelines. No pressure."

She exhaled a shaky laugh, like part of her wanted to believe it could be that simple. "You realize I leave in a few weeks."

"I do." I smiled, but it felt a little too sad. "Doesn't mean I'm not going to enjoy every second I get."

Another pause. She blinked slowly, like she was weighing the risk of saying yes when everything in her screamed *no* in order to protect her heart.

"I'm not asking you to stay," I said. "I'm asking you not to leave tonight."

That finally got her. A quiet beat passed before she reached for the gear shift but kept it in park.

When she looked at me again, her voice was soft, but her words hit like a shot of adrenaline. "I'm not sure I know how to stay. But I don't want to run either."

Emotion clogged my throat. "Then that's enough for me."

We sat there, side by side, not moving, just breathing in the kind of quiet that held possibility. And when she finally reached for my hand, I curled my fingers around hers like I'd been waiting since we were sixteen.

Maybe I had.

**21 /
emily**

I woke from a restless sleep, the memory of Ted's kiss still imprinted on my lips. His solid hand on my face. The way he pulled me in like he had every intention of making up for lost time. A shiver raced down my spine.

Eddie. My first kiss, Eddie.

Ted.

I rolled over, pulling the covers over my head to block out the too-bright morning light. I had forgotten to pull the shade, but it didn't matter. I was wide awake, reliving the past. That summer. That kiss. That boy who had made me feel special, like I belonged.

I fluffed my pillow, staring up at the vaulted ceiling. What if I had met him at the dock like we'd planned? Would we have kept in touch? A ridiculous thought. We were just kids. Of course we would have gone our separate ways. College. Jobs. Life. No need to romanticize it.

And yet, as I brushed my fingers over my cheek where his whiskered jaw had scraped across my skin, heat crept up my neck. I had been the one with his phone number. He didn't have mine. I could have reached out.

But I hadn't.

Because back then, I had made a choice. Keep the peace.

Stay in line. Be the responsible one. I had spent a lifetime doing the right thing. Making sure Mom and Grandma had nothing else to worry about. Keep cool until Sammie and Trevor got settled in their new life.

My phone rang on my bedside table, startling me out of my spiraling thoughts. I reached over, feeling for it blindly. My fingers found the cool solid plastic, and I lifted the phone to my face. Dylan's name came into focus on the screen.

"Morning," I said cheerily, happy to chat with someone from my old life. "Shouldn't you be dropping the baby off at daycare?"

That was how Dylan and I often chatted, starting a conversation in the middle.

The baby babbled away in the background.

"As a matter of fact, we are on our way now."

I sat up and ran a hand through my hair. "To what do I owe the pleasure?"

Dylan told me he generally devoted his car rides with the baby to playing and singing the likes of Ozzy Osbourne and Kiss to offset her mother's Taylor Swift and Sabrina Carpenter obsession. I considered myself honored to get a call.

"Yeah, we're gonna make this quick because I think the baby likes 'Crazy Train.'"

"Goodness." Sitting on the edge of the bed, I stretched my legs out in front of me. The bedroom was so small my toes touched the wall.

"I got a text this morning from Julian Vanderburg. He asked me to fill in with a client this afternoon. And you want to know why…?" The way Dylan dragged out the last word suggested he had some tea to spill. Tea I wasn't sure I wanted to hear.

"I'm sure you're going to tell me," I said, forcing a flippant tone even though my Spidey senses tingled.

"He said he had a last-minute interview he couldn't miss.

I'm supposed to keep it on the down-low." It sounded like he was adjusting the phone and talking to the baby. Then, more clearly, he said, "But of course, that doesn't include you."

"Of course not." I closed my eyes and drew in a deep breath. "You think it's with Blue Moon?" I muttered. Of course it was. We had both been gunning for similar positions. "I am going to freak if they offer him my job." I scrambled off the bed to grab my laptop off the chair where I'd left it.

"I thought the official offer was pretty much a formality?"

"I thought so too." I knelt down on the floor and fired up my laptop and cursed under my breath. If I lost this job…

"Well, where do you currently stand with them?" Dylan asked.

In the background his baby made happy singing noises that were at odds with the panic bouncing around my head.

I opened the email app. "I guess I should reach out to them." Perhaps I had been too cocky, thinking I was an asset they could ill afford to lose.

"Sorry, Emily. Didn't mean to ruin your Friday. Maybe I'm wrong. But I also didn't want you to be blindsided."

"I appreciate it. Now go bark at the moon with Ozzy." I forced a cheery tone I hardly felt.

"Impressive, I didn't think you listened to my music."

"I don't." But I was well enough immersed in pop culture that I knew Ozzy Osbourne.

Dylan made an exaggerated sigh of disgust. "Now go find out what's going on."

"Thanks, Dylan." I ended the call, scanned my emails, and froze when I saw an unread message that had landed in my inbox sometime yesterday evening. *I silenced my phone during the holiday concert.* I missed the new email alert. I'd only turned the phone off silent mode before flopping into bed, my mind still tangled up with thoughts of Ted's lips.

Darn it.

The email was from the hiring manager at Blue Moon, requesting I complete another case study, the dreaded hurdle to jump during an interview. One I thought I had already leapt over.

They wanted it first thing tomorrow morning. On a Saturday. My heart sank.

I quickly showered and dressed and headed downstairs, both surprised and relieved to find Cookie in the kitchen.

She looked up from rolling out the dough for cinnamon buns. "Morning, sleepyhead."

My watch said seven-thirty. The bakery opened at eight. "I didn't expect you here this morning. I thought maybe you'd be tired after your night out."

Cookie lifted an eyebrow. "Oh, I'm not dead yet." The underlying humor in her tone made me not want to press with any more questions. She was allowed her privacy, and I wasn't sure I wanted to know any more about my grandmother's date with Big Ed.

"I'll get the coffee going." I slipped into the front of the bakery and prepped the shop.

I opened the doors promptly at eight, and next thing I knew it was after ten. The morning rush was dying down. I felt an odd sense of satisfaction with the work, much as I had as a little girl when Cookie paid me a dollar an hour. A kid didn't need much money to feel rich. The memory made me smile. Yet I was anxious to hide away with my computer to work on the case study.

Once the morning crowd cleared out, I found Cookie in the kitchen, wiping down the stainless-steel counters like she was prepping for a Health Department inspection.

"Any chance you could cover the shop?" I asked, trying to sound casual and not like I was one breath away from hyperventilating. "I've got some work-work to do."

"Work-work?" Cookie's brow lifted, but before I could

backpedal, she shook her head and smirked. "Sure thing. I'll text you if we get slammed."

"Thanks," I said, already pivoting for the stairs.

I jogged up to the apartment, the chill from the stairwell clinging to me until I settled into the cozy chair beneath the window. I pulled my laptop onto my knees and opened the case study file.

My shoulders locked up like I was prepping for battle. Which, in a way, I was. Another case study. Another obstacle. The dream job I'd already pictured on my LinkedIn profile now felt not so "sure thing." Like someone had snuck in overnight and moved the goalposts.

I inhaled slowly. I could do this. I'd done harder things. Financial modeling, C-suite presentations, surviving the past three Christmases alone in my Pittsburgh apartment because I had to work. This was just numbers and logic. This was my thing.

Still, I stared at the blinking cursor, and my mind—traitor that it was—drifted. To last night. To Ted. His smile when he handed me that fantastic meatball sub. The way his hand felt when he brushed hair from my cheek. The kiss.

Goodness, that kiss.

My stomach fluttered, and I shook my head, gently tapping my face, as if slapping sense into myself. Nope. Not today. This was not the time for wistful daydreaming. I was this close to landing a role I'd been working toward ever since I realized I was good at numbers.

I opened the file and forced my eyes to the text. *Focus, Emily. Flirting with the boy-next-door-turned-man-of-your-forgotten-dreams might make your heart do a weird little dance, but it isn't going to land this job.*

Still, my lips tingled.

Focus.

You can melt down later. Right now, you have a case study to crush.

emily

I made sure to save the file and looked up from my computer, surprised to see that the small apartment was cast in heavy shadows. When did it get so late?

I let out a long breath and rolled back my shoulders. I closed my laptop and rushed downstairs. Cookie closed the register and picked up a canvas bank tote.

"Ah, there she is," Cookie said, in that sweet, welcoming tone that had always made me feel nostalgic, even when I was a kid. "I thought you might have gotten lost up there."

I scratched my head and looked around. "You closed up shop?"

"Just like I've done for fifty years."

"I'm sorry. I got wrapped up in work."

"I thought you had the month of December off." Cookie put the bank deposit down and rested her hand on it.

"I do. However, the job I thought I had wanted me to do another case study."

Cookie pursed her lips. "So, they make you do work before they hire you? I should try that. Might get to relax a bit around here."

"It's common in my industry." I hated the defensiveness

that had crept into my tone. "They want to make sure they hire the right person."

If Cookie wondered why I had said I already had a new job when, apparently, they were still interviewing, she never said boo. She always seemed to know the right thing to say—or not to say in this case.

I scratched my head. "Where's Maddie? I thought she was taking the bus here after school."

"She did. But she left a little while ago. She has a basketball game to cheer at tonight."

"Oh, are you going?"

"A certain gentleman asked me if I'd like to." Cookie's youthful smile warmed my heart. I loved that she didn't just go home and watch TV. She flicked her fingers in a shoo gesture. "Go double-check the front door while I finish up here."

As I made my way through the front of the bakery, I realized Cookie hadn't left much for me to do. She had already hit all the lights save for the soft lighting in the dessert case. Outside seemed a little brighter than usual, and when I reached the entrance, I understood why. Twinkling white lights around a strand of garland framed the doorway of the shop. I stepped outside, wrapping my arms tight around my middle against the winter chill. The front of the store reminded me of something you might see in the Strip District in Pittsburgh during the holidays.

Cookie appeared at the front door, a look of delight on her face when she held out the big black puffy coat that hung by the back door. The same one we grabbed to go outside for deliveries.

"You like?" she asked as she helped me stuff my arms into the long coat.

"It's beautiful. Who did this?"

She lifted a pale eyebrow, and her bright-blue eyes shifted

behind me. I turned around to find Ted standing there with a wreath hooked on his arm.

"The pièce de résistance," he said before placing it on a hook next to the door.

"You did this?" I asked, aware that Cookie was lingering inside the door, watching for a few moments before disappearing.

"This was your vision, right?"

"That was before I realized you weren't a handyman for hire." I hugged the bulky jacket around me. "But yes." I studied the decorations. "I recognize some of the items I ordered online."

Ted extended his hand, and for a moment, I hesitated. Then I slipped mine into his, and heat curled up my arm like a lit fuse. His palm was warm, steady. The memory of his hands cradling my face, the press of his lips against mine, came rushing back, stealing the air from my lungs.

"And look how well the decorations go with the brewery next door. It's one giant masterpiece."

From the curb, the decorations on the front of the brewery complemented the new ones on the bakery.

"It looks fantastic. It really does."

Ted grabbed his cell phone and showed me some photos. "I posted this on our socials and put on the hashtag for the town competition. You can share it on the bakery's page if you want. But consider yourself entered in the town contest for best-decorated business on Main Street."

I chuckled. "You're not worried about the competition?"

"I welcome it!" He held his chin up, looking every bit as confident as someone could look in that silly hat. "Have you had dinner? Are you hungry?"

As if in response to his question, my stomach grumbled. "I am."

He hooked his arm around the crook of mine. "Come on. We have some great chili on the stove."

I glanced through the bakery window and spotted Cookie waving me off with a knowing little smile. Of course she was in on this. Every bit as much as Ted. My jaw tightened. Was she secretly rooting for me to stick around Walleye Point? The idea was absurd. What would I even do here? Help my sister run the bakery? Host trivia night at the brewery? My job—goodness, I prayed I'd still have a job—was in Pittsburgh.

"Okay," I said, resigned. A person needed to eat.

Ted yanked open the door of the brewery, releasing the scent of hops and grilled food. The place was almost full, despite the weather. The dark hole-in-the-wall bar was now a bright brewery with a full dining room with wood accents.

"Mind sitting at the bar?"

"Not at all." I ran my hand across my hair, wondering what I looked like. I had spent most of the day hunched over a computer and hadn't even looked in the mirror. Even my eyes felt gritty. It was like my entire body was revolting against its return to the laptop.

Ted leaned in close to me, his minty breath whispering across my cheek. "You look great." It was like he read my mind. *He* really looked good.

I slid onto a stool, doing my best to play it cool.

A woman who looked to be about ten years older than me offered a weary smile. She was probably tired of dealing with customers all day. She set coasters in front of us. "What can I get you?"

I picked up the coaster and turned it over in my hands, studying the Top Shelf logo of a hockey net and crossed hockey sticks. "What do you recommend?"

She held up her finger then came back with two beers. "My favorite."

"Hey, Galina," Ted said, "this is Emily Johnson."

Ah. His father's widow.

Galina's lips pressed into a firm line. "I figured as much." She wiped her hands on the white apron knotted at her waist.

For a second, I thought she might offer a handshake, but instead she planted both palms against the bar like she was bracing herself. "Nice to finally meet you." Her tone was polite but cool, like she was still deciding whether I deserved the benefit of the doubt.

"Nice to meet you too," I said, trying not to sound defensive.

Galina gave a slow nod. "I hear Ted spent the afternoon decorating the front of the bakery."

"He did." I shot Ted a sidelong glance, still not sure how I felt about the surprise. "I had no idea he was going to do it. I was upstairs working." I took a sip of the beer. It was good. "He did a fantastic job."

Galina's eyes stayed on me, sharp and unreadable. "That's our Ted. Always going the extra mile." The words were neutral, but something about the tilt of her head made it sound less like praise and more like a gentle warning.

Or maybe I was just imagining it.

As if on cue, Ted slipped off the stool and tapped my back. "I'll get us some of that chili."

I struggled between my hunger and my panic at being left to an interrogation by this woman who apparently had something against me. Now that I knew who she was, I suspected I knew what that something was. I was the person standing between her and a parking lot for this booming business.

A few more customers arrived and strolled up to the bar. After Galina filled their orders, she made her way back to me. I drummed my fingers on either side of my tall glass, trying to act casual.

"Ted seems to be spending a lot of time with you," Galina said, apropos of nothing.

"I guess it's a small-town thing," I said evenly.

"I suppose. How's your sister doing?"

"She's on the mend. Thanks." I prided myself on my conversational skills, yet I struggled to keep this one going.

"How's business?" Galina's voice cut through the din, her gaze sweeping the full dining room like she'd personally invited every patron here. "The bakery always seems quiet."

"Business is fine," I said, forcing my tone to land somewhere between cordial and clipped. My eyes darted to the kitchen, silently begging Ted to return.

She wasn't done. "You're throwing all your money into that place. Can you really afford that?"

My pulse thudded in my ears, signaling the same slow burn that crept up whenever one of the finance bros questioned me, as if just by virtue of being a woman, I wasn't qualified. I clenched my jaw and smiled, the kind of smile that never reached my eyes.

She probably still carried a grudge from the days Ted's dad tried to edge the bakery off the block. I had no doubt my name came up. Sammie wasn't exactly known for subtlety.

I folded my hands calmly on the bar. "The bakery's been in our family for seventy-five years. Helping them out wasn't simply a business move. It was personal. You understand that."

Galina studied me like I was a riddle she hadn't decided whether she wanted to solve. "I do. And your sister seems to think you have bottomless pockets." She looked past me, and I turned to find Ted emerging from the kitchen, carrying two trays.

He was a beautiful, chili-bearing distraction.

"I'll let you eat." Galina gave the bar a brisk pat and turned toward the two customers at the far end, her exit mercifully swift.

Ted slid onto the stool beside me, smiling in that way that made me melt. "As promised."

My stomach rumbled, and I took a big bite of the cornbread on the side. "This is good," I mumbled behind my hand.

"Told you."

I leaned in and whispered, "I don't think your stepmom likes me."

"Don't take it personally. My dad wanted the whole block. The bakery was the lone holdout."

I shot him a look. "Is she going to hold a grudge forever?"

He held up his palm, as if he had no way of knowing. "The chili was worth coming in, though, right?" he asked, watching me lift the spoon to my mouth.

I turned slightly on the stool, watching him from the corner of my eye. I really didn't want to like this guy.

But I did.

And unless I planned to hole up upstairs for the rest of my time in Walleye Point, I couldn't avoid him forever.

"So," Ted said casually, adding sour cream to his bowl, "any chance you want to come to the basketball game? I hear it's where all the cool kids are going."

His voice was light, and his gaze lingered on mine. And something about the way he asked, so hopeful, so utterly innocent, made my stomach flip.

I should've said no. I should've stuck to my plan of proofreading the case study one more time and, most importantly, drawing a clear boundary with Ted. The more time I spent around him, the harder it became to ignore my growing feelings for him.

But instead, I heard myself say, "Yeah. I'd love to see Maddie cheer."

And I meant it.

And if I was being honest with myself, I wasn't quite ready to say goodnight to Ted.

23 /
ted

The squeaking of sneakers on the polished gym floor floated above the excited din of the Walleye Point community. Basketball was the one popular sport that I hadn't played. Yet even as a teen, I liked joining the crowd and getting lost in something where no one expected anything of me.

As we made our way toward the crowd, I let my hand hover over Emily's lower back, wanting to give her room and yet not wanting any space between us. Big Ed and Cookie sat in the front row of the bleachers, their heads tipped in conversation, much as they had been last night at the concert. My grandfather had insisted on driving Cookie alone, perhaps not wanting to feel like his great-grandson who had to ride in the back seat of my truck with his date.

Upon seeing them, Emily rushed ahead and gave her grandmother a kiss on the cheek. The older woman shifted a bit on the bench to make room for us. It would be a tight fit.

"How about we go up in the bleachers?" I asked. "Get a better view?"

Emily looked up and smiled then said something to Cookie. We climbed the wooden bleachers, finding seats at the very top. The best perk was that we could lean against the cinderblock wall.

"So, what do you generally do on a Friday night in Pittsburgh? Go to a Penguins game? Maybe a Pirates game in the summer? Grab a few beers after?"

Emily drew in a deep breath and released it, an amused expression brightening her face.

"The world, my friend, does not revolve around sports and beer."

I tucked my chin in feigned confusion. "What do you mean?"

Turning her focus to the row of cheerleaders along the wall under the scoreboard, which indicated that the away team was up by six, she asked, "Did you ever consider how much time sports consume?"

"You act like that's a bad thing."

"I suppose it depends on your interests."

One of the players threw a shot, and it bounced off the rim.

"Come on, Lakers!" I yelled.

Emily bumped my shoulder with hers. "I've heard of the LA Lakers, but what exactly *is* a Laker?"

"A person who lives by a lake?" I was making the answer up as I went along, but it sounded good. I pointed down to Big Ed. "Look at our grandparents, living their best lives."

Emily dragged her lower lip through her teeth. "They look happy."

I watched Cookie and Big Ed for a long moment, wondering when their relationship had shifted from companionship to something more. Had it always been there, quietly growing while the rest of us were too wrapped up in our own lives to notice? The whirlwind of launching the brewery had consumed most of my time, especially during those first months after I returned to Walleye Point.

"Cookie was there for him after Dad died," I said. "My grandfather said more than once that a father should never outlive his son. He kept a stiff upper lip, but the loss devastated him."

"It is so hard to lose someone you love. Cookie lost her daughter when she was a young adult. I imagine she was able to relate. Help him through it." Emily ran a hand across her jaw, as if deep in thought. "I'm glad they found one other."

The crowd erupted in cheers, shattering the moment of connection. One of the players had scored a three-pointer. I cheered without taking my eyes off Big Ed. He had been such a calming force in my life.

Feeling bold, I reached over and pulled her hand into mine. "I'm glad we found each other too."

Emily met my gaze. Pink blossomed on her cheeks. She slipped her hand out of mine and tugged at the zipper of her coat, and I helped her slide it off her arms. Feeling as if I had said too much, I leaned over and made a joke. That's what I always did. "If our grandparents get hitched, does that mean we'll be related?"

Emily playfully slugged my arm with a soft punch. "Gross. And no, we would not be related."

"So, that means I still have a chance?" I tucked a strand of hair behind her ear. Her skin felt fiery hot.

I searched Emily's eyes, and she returned my gaze head-on, steady and unflinching. The row of boys in front of us leapt to their feet, cheering wildly. I seized the moment and brushed the softest kiss across her lips, lingering just long enough for the electricity to spark between us before the crowd settled and left us in full view of the town.

Emily stared straight ahead. Her expression was neutral save for the unmistakable smile tugging at her lips. After a beat, she patted my thigh in what was supposed to be a casual gesture, but it sent a ripple of heat through me.

"Watch the game," she murmured, her tone teasing but firm. "You do remember I'm not big on PDA, right?"

I caught her hand before she could pull away, threading my fingers through hers and bringing them to rest against my leg. I pulled her closer, and my lips brushed the shell of her ear. "Noted."

24 /
emily

The high school gym was filled with a chaotic energy that amped up my own, making me feel jittery. Every time the home team scored, the cheerleaders jumped, their white sneakers kicking up and their pompoms pumping as they hollered the name of the boy who had scored.

Maddie was keeping up, but her smile looked a little too fixed, her arms a beat behind the others. Maybe it was nothing. Or maybe I was too distracted to read it right. I'd blame that on the man sitting next to me. Our fingers were intertwined, as if it were the most natural thing.

What am I doing? I'm leaving in a few weeks. This isn't part of the plan.

Not that I had a real plan anymore. Not when he looked at me like that.

Pull it together, Emily.

I shifted in my seat and slipped my hand free, masking it with a casual stretch. I was here for Maddie, not to go on a pseudo date with a man I had no business falling for. And yet, every time our shoulders bumped, my focus drifted from the game to the man beside me.

"You look deep in thought," Ted said, his voice pitched low over the cheers of the crowd. "That's dangerous."

One side of my mouth tugged up. "I'm always deep in thought."

"Mm-hmm." His palm landed lightly on my thigh, sending another spark coursing through me. "Care to share what's on your mind?"

I didn't. Not really. Not the part where I kept wondering how messy things could get if I let myself fall for someone who made me forget my life was mapped out in a city two hours away.

"Oh, nothing." I shrugged, light and breezy. "Just tired. Long day of work."

"Busy at the bakery?"

"Cookie held down the fort. I was upstairs, hammering out a project for my other job." Just the mention of it tightened the knot in my stomach. "It's for the final round of the interview process."

"The job's not locked in?" His tone was casual, but the flicker of something hopeful in his voice made my heart ache.

"It's just a formality," I lied, trying to exude a confidence I didn't feel. "Most likely." This time my voice was barely a whisper. I shifted in my seat, another question weighing on my mind. "Was it hard giving up your job when you moved back here?"

Ted glanced down at his white sneakers then back at me, as if considering. "Not as hard as you'd think. Sometimes life decides for you, and it takes a while to realize it did you a favor."

His answer made me pause. I wanted to ask more, and a hundred questions pinged around my head, but the one that came out was simple. "How did it do you a favor?"

He smiled softly. "Because now I get to be part of Jayden's life. But even if he wasn't part of the equation, I'd still say it was the right move. Before, I had a great job, but

I'd come home exhausted, unsatisfied. Now, I work harder than I ever have, but it feels like I'm building something that's my own."

I relaxed my gaze, watching the blur of movement on the court. "What if I make the wrong choice?" I turned to find him watching me, his attention unwavering.

"About?"

"Everything." I rubbed a hand across my chin. "People are counting on me. If I don't take the job, and the bakery tanks again, I won't be able to bail them out. I'm the fallback plan."

"Do you like the job?" he asked gently.

I hesitated. "I'm good at it."

"That wasn't the question." He reached over and hooked his pinky with mine. His touch was grounding in the best way. "If you could do anything, no expectations, what would it be?"

I opened my mouth, but nothing came out. "I don't know." And that scared me more than I wanted to admit. The longer I stayed in Walleye Point, the more something was shifting. I could feel it. This place was starting to feel like mine too. "What if I let everyone down?"

"What if your sister's stronger than you give her credit for?"

Before I could respond with a lifetime of reasons why I'd always needed to be the safety net, the gym erupted. A final buzzer, a half-court shot, and suddenly the crowd was on its feet, surging down the bleachers in a blur of cheers and squeaking sneakers.

I searched the chaos until I found Cookie, calmly seated on the end of the row like she'd seen a hundred buzzer-beaters and none of them fazed her.

Ted looked over at me, his voice low. "Have faith."

I nodded slowly, not totally sure what I was agreeing to, but knowing, somehow, it mattered.

"You ready?"

I slipped my hand into his and let him guide me down the bleachers, my heart not quite sure why it was racing.

Jayden materialized from the crowd and high-fived his uncle. "Did you see that shot?"

"I did. Pure clutch," Ted said, grinning.

I congratulated Jayden then told Ted I'd meet him by Cookie and Big Ed. Sliding into the seat beside my grandmother, I took in the swirling mass of teenagers.

"Great game. Hemsley's first basketball player." Big Ed beamed with pride. "My boy played football. Even coached his son's team."

I turned, catching Ted's expression just before he masked it. I found myself wanting to peel the layers away, to get to know the heart of this man.

"How did Maddie get here?" I asked, an inexplicable worry forming in my mind.

"Her dad dropped her off," Cookie said, rubbing her lower back. "But he left before the third quarter."

My stomach twisted. "He left?"

Cookie winced as she stood, pressing a hand to her hip. "You should check on her. Make sure she has a way to get home."

I spotted Maddie across the gym, her face unreadable as she chatted with a few teammates as they followed the crowd out the door. I sighed and turned to Ted. "I need to make sure she's set."

"I'll wait."

We lingered near the gym doors as the crowd thinned. When Maddie still hadn't appeared, I touched Ted's arm. "I'm going to find the girls' locker room. See what's taking so long."

"I'll be here." He gestured to the opposite hallway.

I was about halfway there when the locker room door flew open and Maddie stormed out, clutching her stuff to her chest like she'd grabbed it in a hurry. She swiped at a tear then froze when she spotted me.

"Oh. Hi." Her brow furrowed, and she scrubbed at her cheeks like she could erase whatever had just happened. "What are you doing here?"

I wanted to ask a dozen questions, but I started with the most pressing. "Your dad left, so I wanted to make sure you had a ride."

Her shoulders sagged. "He left?" Just two words, but they were laced with so much disappointment it made my chest clench.

I nodded, stepping closer. "What's wrong, honey?"

I slipped an arm around her shoulders, but she jerked away, biting her lip. Before I could ask another question, voices echoed down the hall. Someone was coming.

Maddie grabbed my elbow. "Let's go."

"Okay." I glanced over my shoulder to find two girls emerging from the locker room. It might have been over a decade since I was a teen, but I recognized the drama. I fixed a smile on my face. "Let's find Ted. He's our ride."

Maddie seemed to straighten a little. "You came with Jayden's uncle?"

My heart lifted, like I was one of the cool kids. "Let's go find them."

Maddie's mood seemed to pick up a bit.

We found Ted where I had left him. Alone.

"Found her," I said, sounding overly cheery, trying to prop up my niece. I felt every bit of the stress and sadness radiating off Maddie, and I hurt for her. "Is Jayden getting changed?" I glanced around, looking for Ted's nephew. "Maybe we can go for ice cream."

Ted handed over my coat. "Jayden has plans with some friends. He's sleeping over at a buddy's house." He shrugged, as if he wasn't sure what was going on. "We can head out."

Just then, the two girls from the locker room passed us.

One cupped her hand over her mouth and whispered something to the other. Whatever it was, it must've been hilarious because they both burst into laughter.

Maddie stared at the floor, her cheeks burning red.

My jaw tightened. Why did kids have to be so mean?

"We can still go for ice cream," I said, my voice soft, knowing even as I said it that it was the wrong move. Maddie was sixteen, not six. A scoop of mint chocolate chip with a cherry on top wasn't going to fix whatever just happened.

Ted, reading the moment better than I had, stepped in. "Why don't I get the car and pick you guys up at the curb?"

Maddie shook her head, her shoulders stiff. "I don't want to wait in here."

Then, before either of us could respond, she rushed toward the door, leaving me and Ted standing awkwardly, looking at each other.

"She okay?" Ted asked.

I let out a slow breath. "I have no idea."

But I was about to find out.

25 /
emily

In the back seat of Ted's truck, Maddie was slumped over her cell phone. Something on there had her completely absorbed.

"You did a great job cheerleading, honey," I said, grasping for a way to connect. "Do you like cheering for football or basketball more?"

"I don't know," Maddie said noncommittally, not looking up from the screen. "They're both fine, I guess."

Realizing I probably wasn't going to get much out of my niece, I gave Ted directions to her house. But before I finished, Maddie lifted her head. "Aunt Emily, can I stay with you?" Her pleading tone made my heart squeeze. Like she wasn't sure I'd say yes. Like she needed to be anywhere but home tonight.

"Of course," I said without hesitation. "Text your mom and tell her we're having a girls' night at my place." I sat up a little straighter, warming to the idea. "I have extra jammies, and we can make popcorn and watch a movie."

Maddie's thumbs started tapping away on the screen. A few seconds later, she said, "Mom said okay." I didn't miss the way her shoulders loosened, like she also hadn't been sure her mom would give her permission to stay.

"So, heading back into town?" Ted asked, his tone easy, like always. He reached for the gearshift, and I couldn't help but stare at his hand, remembering how he'd taken mine on the bleachers like it was the most natural thing in the world.

That brief, quiet intimacy still lingered in my mind.

Of course, Maddie's teenage drama had dumped a bucket of cold water on any spark that might've caught fire. Probably for the best. A sensible detour.

"Drop us off back at the bakery," I said, probably louder than necessary to mask the thoughts I had no business having. "My niece and I are going to have a girls' night."

With Maddie in the back seat scrolling, Ted and I chitchatted about everything and nothing in particular. It was like we were trying to fill the silence to avoid thinking about what the night might have been. Once at the bakery, I slipped out of the truck and said a hurried, platonic goodbye to Ted before Maddie and I went upstairs to the Airbnb. She took a shower, and I went downstairs to snag some of Cookie's shortbread and popcorn for our movie night.

When Maddie emerged with her long hair wrapped into a towel, her face looked splotchy. "Are you okay, honey?" I asked.

Her lower lip quivered. "I'm fine." Tears filled her eyes, then one spilled over the edge and trailed down her cheek. *She's definitely not fine.* My fingers twitched. I wanted to pull her into an embrace but feared she'd shut down.

She had to open up to me on her own terms.

I tilted my head, giving her space to talk—or not talk. When she didn't, I picked up the remote from the nightstand. "What do you feel like watching?" I gestured to the snacks sitting in the center of the bed. I had already gotten into PJs and made myself comfortable. "We can make crumbs and stay up late."

Maddie climbed onto the bed and propped a pillow behind her back. She pulled her knees to her chest, resting her chin on top of them. "Did you have a lot of friends when you were my age, Aunt Emily?"

Heart racing, I stared at the blank TV screen, careful not to spook my niece. My mind drifted back to my sophomore year in high school. I hadn't been exactly the most open kid, preferring to keep my worries to myself so as not to upset my mom. "I had a few friends, but I mostly spent my time studying or babysitting. I wasn't naturally part of the in-crowd, but your mom would make me feel included." I smiled at the memory. "Your mom's a keeper."

Maddie scoffed. Of course, she'd be critical of her own mother. "My friends are allowed to do stuff I'm not," she muttered. "They're all at some slumber party tonight. I didn't even get invited because they already know my mom would say no to a sleepover if boys were invited too."

A mixed-gender slumber party? I suddenly felt ancient.

"She's just trying to protect you," I said, gently taking Sammie's side.

Maddie tucked her chin tighter into her knees. "I think she's afraid I'll mess up like she did. Like if I make one wrong move, I'll ruin everything."

The hurt in my niece's tone pierced me. I reached out and smoothed a strand of hair behind her ear. "You were a surprise," I said carefully, "but never a mistake. I don't think I'm overstepping by saying you're the best thing that ever happened to your mom. Probably to all of us."

Maddie wiped away a tear. "I wish she wasn't so strict." Ah, the heart of her sadness.

"She has her reasons. But yeah, she can be a little intense." I gave her a soft nudge with my elbow. "Your mom was the social one, the fun one. I was more the stay-home-and-read type. My idea of wild was staying up later than I was supposed to with a flashlight and a book."

That earned me a faint smile, the kind that meant Maddie was trying to remain stone-faced but couldn't quite help it.

"I guess I turned out okay," I said, nudging her again.

Maddie cut me a sideways look. "Aren't you lonely?"

"No." The response came too quickly, as if I needed to be emphatic to prove it was true. "Why do you say that?"

Maddie pulled her shoulders up to her ears. I had a feeling she heard things like that from her mom. I decided not to press. I was just as guilty of judging my sister's life from the outside.

"Never mind." I cleared my throat. "We have to live the life that we want to live. I love having my independence."

"What about Jayden's uncle? Won't you miss him?"

I laughed. "You don't miss anything, do you?"

"You were wearing his hat when you came back to pick me and Jayden up from the after-party."

I giggled. "Caught!"

"So, will you miss him?"

I drew in a deep breath and released it slowly, buying time to find the right words. Then for some reason, I shared the story of how Ted and I had met at the carnival in the town square when we were kids. How I actually stood him up the morning after. I left out the little detail of how her grandma found the pregnancy test in the garbage that day, the one that meant that Maddie was coming into this world. And that from that point forward, I decided I better remain the wallflower so as not to further stress my mom out.

Maddie shifted and tucked her leg under her, holding her shin. "OMG. Does my mom know you hooked up with Ted Hemsley when you were teenagers?"

A wave of prickly heat crept across every inch of my skin. This was not going to stay secret for long. "I wouldn't exactly say, 'hooked up,' but no, I never told your mom."

Maddie jerked her head back. "You and Mr. Hemsley are meant to be. You *have* to stay. You guys need to get married."

"Whoa, whoa, whoa. I think we're getting ahead of ourselves."

"It's possible though?"

I sighed but couldn't shake the smile from my face. "I'm going back to Pittsburgh after the holidays. I have a job there."

Maddie leaned back into the pillows. "It would be nice if you stayed. My mom misses you too."

I reached over and pulled her into a one-armed hug. "I miss you guys too."

The silence stretched between us until finally Maddie scrambled away from my embrace and twisted to face me with crossed legs, carefully pushing aside the plate of snacks. "I thought Jayden liked me too." I gave her space to continue. "But I think he likes Chloe."

The pit in my stomach turned to ice. Ugh, I hated the drama of high school. A million responses bounced around my head, knowing any of them could be met with a roll of the eyes or a rebuttal. I settled on the most honest response and said, "I'm sorry. I imagine that hurts. Is there anything I can do?"

Maddie dipped her head, her long hair falling on either side of her face. She sniffed then looked up with watery eyes. "No. They're all jerks."

I reached out and let my hand rest on her knee. She was wearing my favorite pair of PJs, the soft ones with little cats on them. "I'm here."

Maddie nodded again, perhaps unwilling to speak for fear of breaking down. After a beat, she twisted back around and grabbed the remote and aimed it at the TV. "Want to watch a sappy movie?"

"Sure!" I said, perhaps a little too enthusiastically. I rattled off the streaming services I had set up even though I had yet to watch any TV since I had been here.

I placed the snacks between us while she clicked through a bunch of choices and settled on a classic Sandra Bullock movie. Before she hit play, she said, "Thanks for letting me hang. Mom would have been all over me with questions about why Chloe's mom was allowing boys to sleep over."

Warm affection blossomed in my chest. "You can always hang with me. Whatever you need." I meant it. I wanted to be the grown-up I would've wanted at her age. Someone who wouldn't be judgmental or try to pretend they had all the answers. But I also knew I had a responsibility to keep it real.

"Your mom loves you like crazy," I said gently. "She wants what's best for you. You might be surprised what she'd say if you let her in."

Maddie gave the tiniest scrunch of her nose, clearly indicating she had her doubts.

"It's true," I said, nudging her. "She's my big sister, remember? She doesn't always get it right, but she's doing a pretty amazing job."

I sank back into the pillows, watching as Maddie finally pressed Play. And as Sandra Bullock stumbled across the screen in some impossibly romantic disaster, I made a silent vow that I wouldn't let work keep me from being there for Maddie. The time left before she headed off to college was fleeting.

I wasn't sure how long I'd been asleep, but when I stirred, a different movie was playing, and a strange noise tugged me out of my haze. Muffled at first. Then sharper. A distinct sound I couldn't place.

Not from the TV.

And Maddie wasn't beside me.

A flicker of unease curled in my chest as I pushed back the covers and padded toward the bedroom doorway, blinking against the dim glow of the screen. Maddie must have moved the snacks to the nightstand, out of our way.

"Don't turn on the lights," Maddie whispered urgently. Her voice came from near the window, where she was standing just off to the side, her gaze fixed outside through a tiny gap in the blind.

Something about her tone kept me quiet while I closed the distance.

"What's going on?" I whispered, moving to the other side of the window.

"Don't let them see you."

I pressed my back against the wall and peered out, careful to stay hidden.

Splat. Splat. Splat.

"I think they're throwing eggs at the building," Maddie said, her voice tight with a mix of disbelief and anger.

I pulled back the blind a sliver and squinted through the gap. "Who is that?"

"Stop, they'll see you," Maddie hissed, reaching out but missing my arm.

Too late. An egg smacked the glass with a loud crack, just inches from my face. I jerked back, my heart hammering.

"It's Chloe." Maddie bit the words out, clearly disgusted. "And her friends."

"Why would they do this?"

She held up her phone, and the blue glow lit her face. "She has my location."

There was no waver in her voice now, just quiet fury. Whatever sadness she'd been carrying had morphed into something stronger.

"That's enough," I said. "I'm going down there."

Maddie caught my wrist this time. "Please don't, Aunt Emily. I'll never live it down." Her quiet plea stopped me cold.

I peeked out again. A figure lingered in the shadows.

"Is that…?" My breath caught as he stepped into the light.

Jayden.

A sinking feeling settled low in my stomach. I turned toward Maddie. Her eyes met mine for half a second as the truth registered. She bolted to the bathroom, the door clicking shut behind her.

I stood frozen, fists clenched at my sides. Every instinct screamed at me to storm outside and unleash the kind of fury only an overprotective aunt could deliver. But Maddie had asked me not to.

And she was the one who had to face these kids in the halls on Monday.

I hovered by the window, weighing options I knew I wouldn't take. Call Ted? It felt like tattling. Grab a carton of eggs and return fire? Tempting, but not exactly mature.

No, this wasn't about me.

As much as I wanted justice, what Maddie needed right now was for me not to make this worse. I blew out a breath, stepped away from the window, and whispered to the closed bathroom door, "I'm still here."

Even if she didn't answer, I hoped she heard me.

"You seem to be spending a lot of time with Emily," Big Ed said, his voice casual but his eyes sharp. We were both up way past our bedtime, but I'd found I had trouble sleeping when Jayden was out.

I popped a piece of popcorn into my mouth, chewing slowly while debating how much to say, because whatever I said would undoubtedly make its way back to Cookie and then to Emily. Still, I couldn't stop reliving the events of tonight, her hand in mine, our shoulders pressed together in the back row like we were sixteen again. Something about being with her made everything feel easy. Familiar. Like maybe I'd actually find everything I've ever wanted in life right here in Walleye Point. Emily insisted she wasn't staying, but I couldn't help but be hopeful.

Or maybe I'm a darn fool.

Big Ed drummed his fingers on the arm of the recliner, his attention firmly back on the Sabres highlights playing on TV. Our relationship, it seemed, revolved around watching one sporting event after another, interrupted by the occasional "So, how's everything going with Emily?"

"Darn shame we missed that Sabres game," I said, purposely sidestepping his question.

"Glad the Sabres won. It's about time," Big Ed muttered. He, like the entirety of Western New York, was forever strapped in for the emotional rollercoaster that was Buffalo sports.

When the show cut to commercial, he planted both hands on the recliner's arms and twisted to look at me, his expression unreadable. "You avoiding the question?"

"Was there a question in there?" I asked, feigning innocence.

Half of Big Ed's mouth curled in a knowing grin. "I hear Emily is pretty career focused."

I pressed my lips together and nodded. "Nothing wrong with that." Except if it meant her leaving town.

Big Ed looked like he was gearing up for another well-placed remark when my phone buzzed from the other room. Normally, I'd ignore it, but not with Jayden out.

I stood, that flicker of hope sparking before I even saw the screen. Maybe it was Emily.

It wasn't.

The photo of Jayden in his hockey uniform I used for his caller ID was on the screen. I swiped to answer. "Hey, bud. Everything okay?"

"Hey, Uncle Ted." My nephew's tone made me feel like I had a rock in my stomach.

"Everything okay?" I repeated, turning my back to the family room, as if that would allow me to hear better over the sports analyst. Big Ed had a habit of turning up the volume click by click as the evening wore on. On the other side of the line, I could hear shouting and cheers. When Jayden didn't answer right away, I said, "I can come get you. Where are you?" We had an understanding that I'd come get him whenever, wherever, no questions asked.

"I'm on Main Street. We're hanging out in front of the brewery."

I ran a hand across my brow. "I'll be there in five minutes."

"Thanks, Uncle Ted."

"Do you want to stay on the line?" I asked.

"No, I'm good. I'm just gonna tell my friends I don't feel good."

"Got it." I ended the call and let Big Ed know I was heading out, and five minutes later, I rolled up to the brewery. The kids scattered like I'd shown up with a siren and a badge.

Jayden waved to the only friend that didn't ditch then lumbered over, got in the passenger seat, and slammed the door closed.

"You okay? Is that Tyler? Does he need a ride?"

"No." The single word came out clipped.

As promised, I didn't press. A few blocks from the center of Main Street, Jayden muttered, "Colton Banks is a jerk."

"Oh yeah?" I gave him room to talk.

"His sister Chloe got mad because of all the time I've been spending with Maddie, and so Colton took it upon himself to get us to egg the bakery."

My stomach dropped. I'd put a lot of time into decorating the storefront, and Emily had been so genuinely thrilled about it. Would this mean the bakery would automatically be out of the running for the Best Decorated Storefront? But that seemed secondary at that moment, so I pushed my feelings aside and kept my voice steady. "Why the bakery?"

Jayden slumped lower in the seat, his fingers balling into fists. "Chloe and Maddie have been friends forever, and they share locations. Like on the Find My app. Anyway, Chloe figured out she was staying over with her aunt." His voice wavered. "I couldn't get them to stop, so I called you."

I exhaled slowly, gripping the wheel a little tighter. "I'm proud of you."

He scoffed. "I don't feel proud of myself. I tried to talk them out of it, but Chloe just kept getting madder, and that made Colton madder. It ticks me off because people always assume I'm the bad kid, but these kids?" He let out a humorless laugh. "They act like they're so perfect, but then they pull stupid stuff like this and get away with it. It's messed up."

I nodded, letting his words settle. "That's rough, buddy. But standing up to them? Calling me? That took guts."

Jayden kept his gaze fixed out the passenger window. "I didn't mean to hurt Maddie like that."

"Do you think they woke up?" My gaze drifted to the clock on the dash. It was definitely too late to text or call without actually waking them up, if they weren't up already.

"I'm not sure."

"We'll figure this out bright and early tomorrow morning," I said, devising a plan.

Jayden exhaled, his posture rigid, like he was bracing for whatever fallout tomorrow would bring. I reached across the console and ruffled his hair, earning a muttered "Dude, stop."

I chuckled. "You know what we're doing first thing?"

He nodded, resigned but determined. "Yeah. Cleaning the eggs off the front of the bakery." The relief in his voice was palpable, like I'd handed him a way to undo what had been done.

My chest swelled with pride. Jayden was a good kid, in spite of everything he had been through. And even good kids sometimes found themselves in bad situations.

But the real measure of a person?

Was what they did next.

T he next morning, I rolled out of bed carefully, not wanting to disturb Maddie. She was curled up on the other half of the mattress, sleeping peacefully, her hair spilling across the pillow. My heart squeezed.

Despite the whirlwind of the past few weeks, I loved spending time with my family. And yet, a familiar pang of worry crept in. My life had always been about forward momentum—private equity deals, meetings, next steps. But here, in Walleye Point, time felt like it was slipping through my fingers. I was actually going to miss all this.

I shook away the thought and did the one thing I had to do that morning. I took my laptop to the chair under the window, did a quick last review of the project I had completed yesterday, and sent it to the hiring manager at Blue Moon.

Whatever will be, will be.

Resigned, I headed for the shower before my brain could spiral into the next thing it decided to worry about—which undoubtedly would be the state of the egg-splattered storefront. Dressed and ready, I padded downstairs, and when I stepped into the bakery, I came to an abrupt halt.

A long shadow stretched across the floor, and for a split

second, my half-awake brain processed it as some kind of intruder situation. Then, my vision cleared.

A pair of legs was partially visible in the window on a ladder propped against the storefront. Down below, Jayden scrubbed egg splatter from the window.

I froze, debating my next move. Back away and let them finish? Offer them coffee? Pretend I hadn't noticed and allow them to rectify a night of bad decisions?

Before I could decide, the person on the ladder climbed down. It was no surprise that it was Ted. He gave me that frustratingly handsome smile through the window. And no handyman task would be complete without his father's trapper hat perched on his head.

My heart swelled at the mere sight of this man. I was in serious trouble.

My first instinct was to bolt into the kitchen, but I decided Jayden couldn't be the only brave one this morning. I pulled my cardigan tighter around my waist, took a breath, and unlocked the front door.

"Morning." My tone was neutral, but even I could hear the unspoken "What's going on here?" lingering in the single word.

Ted hooked an elbow on a ladder rung, all casual confidence. "Morning. We've got a mess to clean up, but we'll be done soon."

I didn't need to ask what happened. I already knew. But Ted didn't know that I knew.

Before I could decide whether to play dumb or call him out, Jayden straightened, a damp rag in his hand, his expression earnest. "I'm really sorry, Miss Emily. I tried to stop my friends... but I'll make sure it's cleaned up."

"I appreciate it, Jayden." I shifted to look up at the front of the store.

Darker spots indicated where they had already put in

some elbow grease to remove the egg splatter. I didn't see any more evidence of the kids' evening of mayhem.

"We fixed the decorations that got messed up too," Jayden said, his shoulders seeming to relax a bit. "You could still win the competition."

"I really appreciate it. Thank you both."

Ted and I locked gazes for a minute. "You're welcome. We should be done shortly."

I was about to go back inside when Maddie appeared at the door, her hair hastily pulled into a long ponytail and sleep lines on her pretty face. She had thrown on yesterday's clothes. She hung back sheepishly.

I turned to Jayden. "Why don't you stop in for coffee and a donut when you're done?"

Jayden nodded, and Ted smiled. "Sounds great. It's been an early morning."

Once inside, Maddie whispered to me harshly, "Why did you invite him in?" She had her arms tightly crossed over her sweatshirt.

"They cleaned up the mess," I said.

"Probably only because his uncle made him." She was clearly still hurt, and she had a right to be.

"Give him a chance," I said gently, nodding toward the window. Outside, Ted was folding up the ladder. "From what we saw, Jayden didn't throw the eggs. Yet he's the only one here trying to make it right."

"We're probably going to lose the Christmas decorating contest too," Maddie muttered, like that was the real injustice in all this.

I couldn't help the small laugh that slipped out. "If it means that much to you, maybe you should go lend a hand."

Maddie rolled her eyes then wordlessly slipped behind the refrigerated dessert case and started the coffee, apparently done with the discussion.

A few minutes later, Ted and Jayden came inside. I invited

Ted into the back room so we could chat while I checked the baked-goods inventory.

"What happened? We heard the kids out front last night. Maddie begged me not to run them off." I smiled. "That might have been a sight."

He tipped his head, as if he was imagining it. "Jayden called me for a ride." He sighed, growing somber. "He got a little bit in over his head. I think one of the girls was jealous that my nephew was hanging out with Maddie."

"It's tough to be a kid." I peeked around Ted to check on the teenagers. They were talking. Maddie was smiling. The tension in my chest eased. "I think they'll work it out."

"Maybe Jayden can do some odd jobs around the bakery to make up for it," Ted said.

I considered it. "He cleaned up the mess. I think we're square."

Ted nodded, seemingly lost in thought. "He's a good kid."

"I can see that." Ted followed my gaze to the bakery, where Jayden was carrying two mugs of coffee over to the table. Maddie had her head in the refrigerated case, probably grabbing some baked goods for them.

"I appreciate your restraint in all this," Ted said.

I reached out and touched his arm, and the solidness of it sent a zing coursing through me. "He's lucky to have you."

Ted's Adam's apple moved in his throat. He took a beat before he answered, seemingly struggling to speak. "I'm lucky to have him." He searched my gaze, something unspoken stretching between us.

Heat flushed my face at the intensity of his gaze. Maddie popped her head in, offering us coffee and saving me from saying something I might regret.

"Black is fine," Ted said as we both turned and headed to the front of the store, my hand brushing against the back of his.

Ted and Jayden didn't stay long. They probably had their own chores, and the bakery was about to open.

Once they left, I turned to Maddie. "How did things go with Jayden?" My need to know overrode my general rule of not prying.

"Good." She shared Jayden's version of events, which mirrored Ted's.

I dragged my lower lip through my teeth. *Good?* I suspected that was all I was going to get, but then she said, "Jayden asked if I wanted to go to the movies tonight."

My eyebrows shot up, but I kept my mouth shut.

"But I told him my mom said I was too young to date."

"Oh?"

Maddie gave a tiny shake of her head. "My mom never said that. Not in so many words, anyway."

We both laughed, knowing full well Sammie would've had a minor heart attack if Maddie had gone on a date.

Maddie tucked a strand of hair behind her ear, her voice softening. "I'm not really up for all the drama. We decided to just be friends. Hang out." The faintest blush crept into her cheeks, hinting that maybe—just maybe—that status was subject to change.

"That's very mature of you." I studied her face, wishing she understood all the wonderful things in life still ahead of her.

"Yeah, I thought so." She ran a hand down her long ponytail and twirled it around her fingers.

I wrapped my arm around her shoulders and squeezed. "I love you, kid." And man, I was going to miss the heck out of her when I left.

28 /

ted

Jayden had been moping around the brewery all morning, half-heartedly wiping down tables and aggressively sweeping crumbs out from under the bar. I couldn't figure out why because Emily had graciously let him off the hook for the egging incident when she could have made a stink about it. He hadn't thrown a single egg, but he had no way to prove it. So, I had no idea why he was miserable.

He only mumbled when I asked him, so I let it go. Apparently, raising a teenager required more patience than I had right now. However, by midday, I'd had enough of the sulking.

"Hey, grab the new box of bulbs from the back," I said, nodding toward the back office. "We'll swap out the broken strand on the front of the bakery."

He muttered something unintelligible but disappeared without argument. Thank goodness for small favors.

Galina emerged from the back with a dish towel in hand, a little smirk tugging at her mouth. "I heard Jayden was part of the bakery egging. I'm guessing Emily gave him a piece of her mind."

I kept my tone even, my gaze on the bar. "Actually, she

went easy on him. Handled it with a lot of grace." Then I said, maybe a little too casually, "Emily's cool like that."

Galina raised an eyebrow. "She made him feel bad first, though, right?"

"Nope. She believed him. Let him make things right and didn't rub his nose in it."

Galina scoffed, but it lacked heat. "She gave your dad grief back in the day. Her and her sister."

I bent down to scoop up some fallen napkins. "It was business. People don't always agree."

"She's turning your head, that's all I'm saying."

I straightened, dusting my hands. "Do you think I lack good decision-making skills? You were married to the man who raised me."

Her lips twitched again, this time with something almost like affection. "I never said that."

"Feels like maybe you did."

"I guess we'll see." She held up her palms before retreating into the back hallway, apparently done with the discussion.

Jayden returned, box of bulbs in hand, his sulking still intact.

"Let's get this over with," I said. "Then we can pretend this whole thing never happened."

He gave a dramatic sigh. "Maddie said no when I asked her on a date. She said she just wanted to be friends."

I paused, waiting for him to meet my gaze. Ah, so that was what had gotten to him. "Hate to break it to you, kid, but that won't be the last time a pretty girl says no."

A shadow of emotion flickered across Jayden's face. "You're not supposed to make me feel worse."

"Thought brutal honesty might earn me some cool uncle points. Besides, you guys have been friends for a while now. That won't change."

He cracked the barest smile, which I took as a win.

"Come on," I said, clapping a hand on his shoulder. "Nothing like a little manual labor to mend a bruised ego."

Once I set the ladder up in front of the bakery, Jayden kept his back to the window, kicking at a chunk of leftover ice. The sun from the last few days had done a decent job melting a good chunk of it.

"Almost done?" he asked, glancing up at me with a little tilt of his head that reminded me so much of his mom it made my chest ache. Every once in a while, I'd get a flash of the sister I grew up with before everything changed.

"Yep. Just hold the ladder."

I carefully stretched to unscrew the base of the broken bulb and twist in a new one. Below me, Jayden stood hunched, looking like a kicked puppy. I was digging through the back of my brain for something encouraging to say when Cookie and Big Ed walked up.

"Look at my two hardworking men." Big Ed's voice boomed, and he puffed out his chest.

"Maybe I could hire them," Cookie said with a wink in my direction. She gestured toward me. "I heard you were pretty handy."

I laughed. Apparently, word had gotten around that Emily had mistaken me for the hired help.

"Um, I'm sorry I didn't stop my friends from egging the bakery," Jayden said, his voice low but sincere.

Cookie placed a hand on his arm. "Don't give it another thought."

He nodded, still not quite meeting her eyes.

"Well, we have something to celebrate," Cookie said, clearly itching to share something. My brain did a quick spin through all the possibilities, and I just kept landing on the same one. Were these two far more serious than any of us thought?

"Let me get off the ladder," I said, screwing in the last

bulb then backing carefully down the rungs, waiting until I was on solid ground until I told them I was ready for the news.

Big Ed raised a gloved hand. Now it was his turn to hold things up. He peeled off the glove, tapped on the bakery window, and waved for Emily and Maddie to come outside.

Now I was really curious.

"Hi, Cookie," Maddie called as she opened the door, grinning. Her smile dimmed just slightly when she saw Jayden, probably mirroring his dejected mood.

Emily pushed out behind her. "What's going on?" Her eyes lit with the same curiosity I was feeling.

Cookie cupped Maddie's elbow. "Sweetheart, go put on a coat." Then she turned to Jayden. "Can you see if Galina's around? She's part of this too."

It felt like we were wrangling a bunch of monkeys, and at this rate, the sun would set, and we'd be standing under the twinkle lights for whatever big announcement these two had planned. I swallowed my impatience, determined not to kill the vibe. Jayden already risked doing that as he watched Maddie go back into the bakery before finally leaving to collect Galina.

Finally, a few minutes later, we were all gathered out front. Cookie even had Sammie on FaceTime, her image a little pixelated but smiling.

"We're so glad you're all here," Cookie said.

"We won best decorated storefront in Walleye Point," Big Ed said, practically bouncing on the balls of his feet. I think he might have stepped on Cookie's lines, but if her twinkling eyes were any indication, she didn't mind.

"That's great," I said, still a little unclear on who exactly won. But since I'd helped both businesses, either way, it was a win.

"It was a tie," Cookie said, clarifying. "Top Shelf Brewery

and the bakery both won. The town's splitting the prize. Turns out the selection committee had toured Main Street yesterday, even before last night's mayhem."

Jayden blushed a little at Cookie's comment.

"Where do I collect my trophy?" I looked over at Emily, who was smiling at me in a way that made me want to earn another one.

"Oh hush," Big Ed said, reaching for Cookie's hand. "In honor of this victory, we want to host a joint Christmas Eve celebration. Family-friendly, open-house style."

Big Ed's gaze swept across the screen, where Sammie could be seen clapping, to Galina, then Emily, and stopped on me. "Since you're the next generation of owners, we want your blessing."

Galina nodded. "It'll be good exposure for both businesses."

"We'd appreciate the extra business," Sammie said on the phone, holding up her wrist. "I should be back on my feet soon. The sprain's already feeling better."

"I'm game," Emily said, her gaze meeting mine. "Sounds like fun."

"You know me. All in," I said.

"Cookie and I will start making plans. We thought we'd do it over shortbread and hot cocoa." Big Ed stepped toward the bakery. "Maybe the kids can help us keep it from being too old-fashioned."

"Sure," Maddie said, clearly excited.

"Of course, Mrs...." Jayden faltered.

"Cookie, dear. Everyone calls me Cookie." She smiled, her eyes twinkling.

"Now that we have that settled," Big Ed said, "let's go inside and get warmed up. I could go for some of that fancy coffee."

"We'll finish up out here first," I said. "I think I see one more broken bulb." I climbed back up to check the strand.

"Hey Jayden, run back into the supply room and grab me another box of bulbs."

Cookie and Big Ed disappeared into the bakery, closely followed by Maddie.

Below me, Galina caught Emily on the sidewalk. "Emily, wait up. I'm…" Galina paused, surprisingly hesitant. "I'm glad this worked out for both of us."

Even from above, I saw Emily's smile. "Me too. It's good for both businesses."

Galina looked a little taken aback as if she had expected an argument. "Right. Well… thanks for not calling the police on the kids."

"Of course. Kids make mistakes."

Galina nodded quickly. "Well, thanks for not making it worse. I might have misjudged you."

Emily said something I couldn't make out, but based on Galina's response, I could tell it was kind. I turned back to the strand, blinking away the sting in my eyes. I wished my dad was here to see all that. His widow was softening, and his grandson was making solid decisions. Sure, there was a ways to go, but my dad would never get to see how any of this turned out. That dulled a little of my happiness.

"Got them!" Jayden called, jogging over with the new box of bulbs.

I stepped down a few rungs to take them from him, just as the bakery door opened again.

"Jayden, looks like we're on game duty for the party," Maddie said, trying to sound casual. "If you're cool with that."

"Um, yeah. I'm cool," he said.

"Maybe when you're done helping your uncle, we can start planning?" There was a note of hope in her voice.

"Sure thing." Jayden stood a little straighter, and his voice suddenly grew deeper.

I glanced down right as he looked up, a huge grin on his face.

This time, I didn't need to guess what was going on. I already knew.

29 /
emily

The week and a half leading up to the Christmas Eve celebration passed in a blur like one of those movie montages where people are all smiles and happily busy with all the prep, but behind the scenes they're running on caffeine and pure adrenaline. Cookie, Maddie, and I churned out dessert after dessert, with Sammie pitching in when she could, making a point of waving around her cast to remind us she wasn't at full capacity when she needed an excuse to sip coffee and scroll.

Ted and I fell into an easy rhythm during this time. He'd stop in for coffee every morning, greeting me with that handsome smile. When the morning rush cleared out, we'd take a walk, picking up supplies for the Christmas Eve party from the hardware store, and some evenings he'd text me from the sidewalk outside, knowing I was probably upstairs obsessing over emails.

Nothing changed the clock. As much as I treasured those moments, the truth lingered at the edges. The more I let myself like him, the harder it became to pretend I wasn't already halfway packed for Pittsburgh. We both knew this, yet we recklessly plowed ahead, spending more and more time together.

Then five days before Christmas, I got the email: Blue Moon Investment Group was officially hiring me. I finally had the offer I thought I had when I originally quit my old job to come here to help my sister. The only catch? They wanted me in the office the day after Christmas to "hit the ground running" once the holidays were over. Of course I could do it. This was my dream job.

And yet, as the days ticked by, a gnawing dread settled in my stomach. I was going to have to give all of this up—late-night baking sessions, spontaneous laughter, the chaotic but oddly fulfilling energy of Walleye Point. At night, I tossed and turned. During the day, I distracted myself with to-do lists and productivity.

I had never felt so accomplished.

And I couldn't bring myself to tell Ted. We continued to spend time together, most of it in a flurry of last-minute party planning with our families. He never pushed, never asked me to define whatever was happening between us. I kept my plans close to the vest, not wanting to dim the holiday cheer. Of course, I told Sammie because she'd have to make plans for my departure. Maddie could work on her Christmas break, and Sammie's cast would come off before the new year. Everything was falling into place. Yet the longer I delayed telling Ted I had an official departure date, the harder it became.

Until it was too late.

Christmas Eve brought unseasonable warm weather and a whole lot of denial on my part. Ted had cleared the sidewalks, set up heat lamps, and transformed Main Street into a festive open-air event that connected the bakery with the brewery. The party was alive with music, conversation, and the intoxicating scent of cinnamon and sugar. I stuck to my role of refilling dessert trays, brewing coffee, and making sure no one went into a sugar coma.

I convinced myself I was doing the right thing. No one

wanted to think about post-holiday plans. That would be like asking Maddie and Jayden if they should be doing homework for the inevitable return to school. No one wanted to be that guy.

So, here I was, two days away from leaving Walleye Point, and I hadn't told the man who filled most of my waking thoughts. As dread knotted my stomach, I busied myself gathering paper cups and dessert plates from the outdoor tables. Sammie appeared beside me, steady on her feet. The only evidence of her skiing accident was the cast on her wrist.

"Man, you should see your face," she said, her voice light. "You got that million-yard stare."

"Just thinking about how successful the event was." I offered a smile that felt brittle.

"It was a hit. And who knew Galina and I would come together for the common good."

"Pigs do fly," I said, happy to have a distraction. Before she could ask me the one question I didn't want to answer, I pivoted. "Too bad Trevor couldn't make it."

Sammie shifted her weight. "He's been swamped, helping the Fergusons build a surprise playset for their grandkids for Christmas. We were lucky we got that slight thaw. He wants to use the extra cash to get Maddie that laptop she's been hinting at."

"He's been taking a lot of side jobs?" My eyebrows lifted, and I started recalibrating my thoughts about Trevor.

"Too many." My sister lifted a shoulder. "But life is expensive."

"It is." I had thought he was a no-show most of the time because he was either on the road or on the couch. "I'm sure the Fergusons' grandkids will be delighted," I said slowly, realizing most of my opinions about my brother-in-law had been shaped by Sammie's offhand comments. I was her sounding board. And maybe I'd let that blur the whole picture. "He's a hard worker."

"Why do you sound surprised?" Then she laughed, realization brightening her eyes. "I really need to stop telling you the worst when it comes to my husband. Goodness knows, he's not perfect—who is?—but he'd do anything for Maddie. And me." Seemed the holiday spirit had made my sister more charitable when it came to Trevor. Sammie tugged at her coat. "I'm going in to help Cookie clean up inside."

"I'll be right there."

But I didn't move. I stood in the golden wash of the setting sun, watching the way the reds and oranges stretched across the sky like someone had taken a brush to the clouds. I hadn't even left, and already I missed this place. Missed what Ted and I could have had if I didn't have my entire life laid out in front of me in Pittsburgh.

Once the sun disappeared and the crowd trickled away to their own Christmas Eve traditions, we carried the leftover desserts over to the brewery for a quiet wind-down with family.

And that was when Cookie—never one to bury a lede— dropped the kind of news that could change everything. "Well, time to step up," she said casually, popping a cheesecake bite into her mouth. "Ed and I are heading to Florida for a few months."

Sammie's jaw nearly hit the table. "Really?"

"Close your mouth, dear. It's not becoming," Cookie said, tapping Sammie's chin like she was a child.

"Can you at least wait until I hire more help?" Sammie asked then turned toward me. "Especially since Emily is leaving Friday morning for her new job."

My stomach lurched. The room went completely still. I became painfully aware of Ted, sitting right next to me. Listening. Processing. I still hadn't told him.

His chair scraped against the floor as he abruptly stood. "Does anyone need a refill?"

I looked up just in time to see the muscle in his jaw twitch, his gaze fixed somewhere across the room.

Jayden chimed in. "I'll have a brewski."

"You'll have a Coke," Big Ed said, and the table burst into laughter, apparently oblivious to the emotional landmine that had just exploded between Ted and me.

I pushed my chair back, my heart pounding, and followed Ted to the bar. He was pouring himself a beer, his expression unreadable. A few half-picked-over pastry trays sat on the bar.

"Hey there," I said cautiously, sliding onto a stool.

"Hey yourself," he said, the reply clipped.

"The party was a big success."

"Sure was." He didn't even look at me.

He moved to walk past me, but I shifted in my seat, reaching out just short of touching him. "Sit down for a second? I want to talk."

He hesitated then finally sank onto a stool, leaving an empty one between us. An unspoken message.

I swallowed hard. "I'm sorry I didn't tell you myself that I'm leaving Friday." My voice cracked, and I bit my lip, trying to keep it together.

His gaze flicked to mine, sharp and assessing. "You're leaving in less than forty-eight hours. When *were* you going to tell me?"

"We were both so busy..." My excuse felt flimsy even before I finished the thought.

He gave a small shrug, making my heart break all over again.

"I'm sorry," I said again, softer this time. But deep down, I knew the truth. I hadn't told Ted I was leaving because I hadn't wanted to give him the chance to convince me to stay. Then again, maybe I was being presumptuous. Maybe that had all been wishful thinking on my part.

"I came to help my sister with the bakery." I realized how cold I sounded. "There's nothing left here for me to do."

If I hadn't been searching Ted's face for some sort of understanding, I might have missed the subtle uptick of his eyebrows.

"I was going to take you skating. Show you how it's done, remember?" Ted asked, tilting his head just enough to let me know he was aiming for a laugh. His go-to when he felt defensive. He smiled, but it didn't quite reach his eyes, like he was testing the waters and waiting to see if I'd call him out on it.

I swallowed hard. "They want me—"

Jayden suddenly appeared. "I'm just going to grab a pop," he said, his posture stiff, perhaps realizing too late that he'd walked straight into something personal.

Ted seemed to snap out of it. "Oh, right. Sorry, bud." He shifted his weight like he was about to stand.

Jayden held up his hand. "I got it," he said quickly, already reaching behind the bar. He popped the tab on the soda can and lifted it in a small salute. "Didn't mean to interrupt."

Jayden disappeared back to the table, and we were alone again. Sort of. The sound of laughter and clinking bottles buzzed in the background, but here, in this tiny pocket of space at the bar, it was just me and Ted.

I forced a breath and tried again. "I should have told you that they want me in the office the day after Christmas."

"Of course they do." Ted's eyes bored into mine, his expression implacable.

"Ted—"

"It's your dream job, right?" His voice was even, careful. "This is what you've worked for." He was using my words against me.

Frustration bubbled up, tangling with the guilt that had

been gnawing at me for days. "That's not fair. You know this isn't easy for me."

A flash of something sparked in his eyes. Anger? Regret? Disappointment? "Isn't it?" He ground the words out. "You always seem to have a true north. No deviation. Not for anyone."

The air between us crackled, something sharp and unspoken stretching thin between us.

I looked down at my hands and twisted the Claddagh ring on my finger. "I should've told you sooner. I didn't want—"

"To ruin Christmas?" He exhaled, shaking his head slightly. "Or to give me enough time to talk you out of it?"

Heat rose to my cheeks. I didn't answer because we both knew the truth. It was easier to convince myself I was doing the right thing without someone challenging me.

Ted let out a quiet laugh, but there was no humor in it. He pushed off the bar and stood, the anger draining out of him. He dragged a hand through his hair and shook his head. "I'm not being fair. You told me right from the start that you were leaving. No one can accuse you of being indecisive."

A heavy silence settled over us as my mind raced with a million things I should have said, but I couldn't settle on any of them. I was afraid I'd lose my resolve.

Then, just when I was sure I'd never know his touch again, he took a step. Not away. But closer. His hand brushed against my arm. His touch was so tender it sent a shiver down my spine. Then he leaned in and pressed a lingering kiss to the top of my head.

I closed my eyes.

"Don't worry about it." His voice was low, steady. He surprised me by picking up one of the apple turnovers. "You confuse the heck out of me, Emily. You go out of the way to make the perfect apple turnover after I tell you they're my favorite, then you tell me you're leaving." He gave a small shake of his head. "I thought I had you read, but I was wrong."

"You've tried one?" I asked, suddenly giggling at the ridiculousness of it all, but glad to have something else to discuss other than my leaving.

His mouth twitched like he wanted to laugh but couldn't quite get there. "They were good. Perfect, actually." He looked at me, then past me, his jaw working. "Like everything about you."

The compliment landed like a punch, and emotion clogged my throat.

He set the turnover on a napkin and slid it toward me. "Go chase your dream."

"Ted, please, don't—"

But he was already stepping away, already headed back to the table where our families sat celebrating Christmas Eve and the success of our neighboring businesses. I sat there with my stupid apple tart and a shattered heart, surrounded by a holiday spirit I could no longer enjoy. And for the first time in a long time, I wasn't sure if going after the thing I wanted was worth more than losing the thing I needed most.

30 / ted

I sat in a wooden church pew, hands clasped in my lap, staring at a nativity scene that was blurring at the edges. It wasn't the sunlight streaming in through the stained-glass windows that was playing tricks on me. It was my complete distraction that made me incapable of focusing on the Christmas morning service.

Emily was leaving tomorrow.

Tomorrow.

Less than twenty-four hours from now, she'd be back in Pittsburgh, maybe heading into her new office with her big, important job, while I stayed in Walleye Point, pretending I didn't feel left behind.

But could I fault her? I stayed in Walleye Point because it was what I had to do. She was chasing a dream job because she was the financial support behind her sister's bakery. No, I couldn't fault her, but that didn't make it any less painful.

A nudge from my right knocked me out of my thoughts.

Jayden grinned at me, far too amused for someone who was supposed to be paying attention. "You good, Tedster?"

I froze mid-exhale and slanted a side eye at him.

Sensing my annoyance, he pressed on. "How about Big T, like Gramps? You know, Big Ed."

Inwardly I shook my head. The odd workings of a teenaged boy's brain. I kept my voice to barely a whisper. "Pay attention to the service."

"As soon as you do," he muttered without moving his lips, like a ventriloquist.

I shot him a look that should have been enough to silence him.

Jayden shrugged, but he wasn't done. He leaned in slightly, keeping his voice low. "I have an idea."

"What?" I kept my voice low, aware of the curious stares drilling into the back of my head from the surrounding pews.

"Ice skating." Jayden's lips twitched. "I heard you and Emily talking about it last night. Seemed like something you really wanted to do."

I clenched my jaw. Replaying my conversation with Emily wasn't something I was up for. And it wasn't so much the skating I really wanted to do, but the hanging out with Emily.

Jayden draped an arm across the back of the pew, way too casual. "Anyway, I was thinking maybe we could start a new holiday tradition this year. Go to the rink. You know, mix it up."

I narrowed my eyes. "Since when do you care about holiday traditions?"

Jayden made a show of being offended, but he was obviously enjoying himself. "Since today."

A little fresh air, a little movement might do me some good. Anything to quiet the noise in my head.

"Want to go right after church?" I asked.

Jayden twisted his lips, as if debating something. He pulled out his phone and checked it surreptitiously by the side of his thigh. Man, couldn't he leave the phone alone for an hour? "Yeah, let's go after church. Sounds good."

I mostly agreed to keep him quiet.

Jayden rushed me, Big Ed, and Galina out of the church immediately after the service. If Emily and her family were here, I didn't see them. Then we grabbed our skates, and my nephew hurried us out the door, as if the rink was going somewhere.

When we reached the town square, we weren't alone. And that was when I really knew something was up.

Emily was already there.

My racing heart thudded loudly in my ears. She stood near the edge of the ice rink, bundled up in a soft gray coat, her brown hair tumbling in loose waves around her scarf. And next to her was Maddie.

I shot a look at Jayden and his goofy grin. *Jayden and Maddie are in on this.* I closed my eyes for a beat. How had I walked straight into this? And judging by the flicker of surprise in Emily's eyes, she hadn't seen it coming either.

Jayden clapped a hand on my shoulder. "Look who's here. A total coincidence." His tone suggested that, in fact, it was not a coincidence.

I turned my head slowly, not bothering to hide my skepticism. "Uh-huh." I pointed at Cookie, Big Ed, Sammie, and Trevor making their way across the street. "And the rest of the family arriving is purely good timing."

Jayden gave me an innocent smile. "Apparently everyone wants to start a new tradition."

Before I could fully process what was happening, Maddie waved at us. Her grin was wide, sweet, and just calculated enough to remind me she wasn't nearly as innocent as she appeared.

When Emily caught me watching her, she gave me a tight, apologetic smile. Despite how things had ended last night, she didn't exactly look disappointed to see me. That was something.

With a resigned sigh, I stepped forward. "Well, this is subtle."

Emily's cheeks were pink from the cold. "I don't suppose teenagers have learned the art of nuance."

I laughed, the tightness in my chest loosening just a fraction. "I suppose not."

"Since you're both here…" Maddie grinned, pulling a pair of skates out of her bag for her aunt. "Might as well make the most of it."

Emily shot a look at her niece. "Where did these come from?"

Maddie batted her lashes. "Christmas magic."

I shook my head. "Where exactly did you think you were going? Jayden, at least, had the sense to make us all go home after church for warmer clothes and our skates."

"Maddie dragged us out for batteries," Sammie said, appearing beside Trevor, her arm looped through his. "And speaking of errands, we're headed to the drugstore. I actually do need a few things, and I'm not up for breaking another bone."

"You're not staying to watch us make fools of ourselves on skates?" Maddie asked, only half joking.

"As tempting as that sounds," Trevor said, pulling Sammie a little closer, "it's freezing out here."

Cookie chimed in, joining their little group. "I bet your mom's not freezing her tush off on that Mediterranean cruise."

"Can we do a cruise next Christmas?" Maddie asked hopefully.

"Start saving your pennies," Sammie said in true mom form.

"I don't think there are enough odd jobs in Walleye Point to fund that," Trevor said.

"You could all come visit Big Ed and me in Florida," Cookie said, already shivering. "Ed and I are going to take our thermoses of cocoa over there." She pointed to a bench across the way. "And you two," she said, waving her red mitten between Emily and me, "figure this out." There was no mistaking what *this* was.

Emily's eyebrows lifted. "I'm not sure how I feel about this." She lowered her voice in an attempt not to be overheard.

"Yeah, me neither," I said, though my heart said otherwise.

"Oh, please," Big Ed said with a huff. "You'll both be thanking us later."

Maddie dropped Emily's skates onto the bench before she and Jayden headed to the opposite side of the rink. A not-so-subtle exit.

"Good thing I dressed for the walk," Emily muttered, pressing her fuzzy pink hat down over her windswept hair. Her cheeks were flushed, and her eyes held that uncertain glint again.

Just live in the moment.

"You even have your own hat. What do you say? One last Walleye Point adventure before you trade all this in for corporate coffee and your very own cubicle?"

Emily laughed. "You make it sound so glamorous."

"Just calling it like I see it."

She let out an exaggerated sigh. "Fine. But if I wipe out, you're responsible. I'm not showing up to my new job in a cast. It doesn't pair well with heels."

"I'll think about it," I said, already planning to catch her if she so much as wobbled.

We both sat on the bench to lace up our skates. The kids had already put theirs on and gotten on the ice. Maddie was taking each glide gingerly while Jayden was literally skating circles around her, his hockey skills on full display. How in the world did that kid have time for three sports? When one of Maddie's skates came out from under her, my nephew swooped in and caught her before she fell. She squealed in what sounded like a mix of delight and fear. He hooked his arm around her elbow, and they made their way around the rink again.

Smooth, kid. Smooth.

I watched them for a second then exhaled, my breath visible in the cold air. "Kinda wondering if they did this for us or them."

Hesitancy clouded Emily's otherwise bright-blue eyes. "Maybe both. This might be partly my fault. I told Maddie about the summer we missed each other at the dock."

"It might be my fault. Jayden overheard me mutter something about ice skating when we were talking at the bar last night."

Last night.

Still bent over my laces, I said, "I'm sorry for how that ended. I was just…" I hesitated, looking for the truth without saying too much. "Disappointed."

Her fingers paused mid-tie, her glance drifting to me. "You had every right to be. I should've told you sooner that I was leaving."

I sat up straight. "Truce?"

Emily straightened, her gaze locking with mine. It was open but still carried that flicker of uncertainty. "Truce," she said softly. She bit her lower lip, like she was weighing whether to say more. "I like to act like I have everything figured out. But I really don't."

It hit me, the honesty behind her words. Like she was handing me a piece of herself she rarely let anyone see. "None of us do," I said, keeping my voice low.

She tilted her head, and for a second, the mask slipped. The one she wore when she had to be the strong one, the one who solved things, carried the weight, kept it all together. Vulnerability wasn't something that came easy to her.

I reached out, brushing her arm gently. "You don't have to pretend with me."

Her eyes searched mine. Then she gave a small nod, her throat working as she swallowed.

"Maybe," I said, covering her hand as it rested on the

bench between us, "we just focus on what's right in front of us." I arched a brow. "It is Christmas, after all."

Emily looked over at me. "Merry Christmas, Ted." Something in her expression made hope spark at my core. It wasn't quite a promise, but something close. Something that let me know she hadn't locked the door on us.

"Merry Christmas, Em."

Emily searched my face then broke into a huge smile. "All right, let's see if you can really skate as well as you claim you can." She stood, wobbled dramatically, and dropped right back onto the bench with a laugh.

I gave her a look. "Graceful."

"Hush, you."

I stood and held out a hand, a slow grin tugging at my mouth. "Come on. You can't overthink it."

She stared at my hand then up at me. Something charged passed between us. I felt like this was a pivotal moment.

31 /
emily

I swallowed, my fingers tightening on the edge of the bench, afraid to take his hand. Afraid I wouldn't want to let go. I hadn't intended to reopen this door. Ted and I had said our goodbyes last night, such as they were. It definitely felt like we had a lot of unfinished business, but it didn't matter.

"Come on." Ted coaxed me again. "I won't let you fall."

"Yeah, um, yeah, okay." I shook away all the doubts crowding in on me and accepted his hand. Even through the gloves, a warmth shot up my arm, inviting, electric. *Oh man, this door isn't just open, it's flung wide open.*

I stood a little too quickly, grimacing when one of my ankles bent, and he clutched my hand tighter, not allowing me to fall. I believed him when he said he'd never let me fall.

Ted led me across the snowy path to the rink while I did my best not to wipe out before we even hit the ice. The teenagers kept to the far end of the rink, talking to their grandparents, who were sipping cocoa out of their thermoses. Something about watching Cookie and Big Ed's relationship over this past month—a relationship they had probably been skirting around for years—made me realize that time was fleeting. No one was promised forever.

Goodness, way to dull the bright, shiny day.

"Ready?" Ted asked when we reached the boards edging the rink. Someone had shoveled the snow from the rink, making it passable at best. The warmer temperatures probably did a number on the surface, but the frigid evening temperatures kept it solid. Either way, the teens seemed to be having no trouble.

"Ready as I'll ever be."

Ted stepped up onto the ice, spun around to face me, and grabbed hold of both of my hands, helping me over the boards. Skating backward, he guided me a few feet in, our skates rumbling over a patch of bumpy ice.

I felt like a newborn giraffe trying out my new legs while Ted looked like he had been born on skates. All those years of playing hockey. He let go of my hands, and I stood rooted in place. He made an easy circle around me, grinning. "You need instructions?"

"I need a Zamboni to smooth out all the bumps in this ice." I inched forward like I was stepping through a minefield.

Ted bit back a laugh. "Come on. Give me your hands."

I sighed dramatically, like I thought this was the worst possible idea, but placed my hands in his. Placed my trust in him. He pulled me forward, effortlessly gliding backward as I stumbled, my toe pick digging into the ice.

"Center your weight on the middle of your foot."

"How about don't fall on your backside," I grumbled.

"Yeah, that too." He glided toward the center of the ice, easily pulling me along.

"See?" he said, his voice teasing. "You're doing great."

"That's in the eye of the beholder," I muttered, frustrated that I couldn't seem to get my feet solidly under me. *If that isn't an apt metaphor for my life.*

For a few minutes, we just skated, Ted going from holding both of my hands to one. The air was crisp, and big fat snowflakes fell from the sky. It was the perfect Christmas setting. Meanwhile, Maddie and Jayden zipped past us at full speed, their laughter echoing in the cold air.

And for once, my brain was quiet.

Not racing with deadlines. Not calculating exit strategies.

Just here. In the moment.

With Ted.

I teetered, and Ted pulled me closer, wrapping his arm around my waist to steady me. Then he spun around to face me. "This is where we had our first kiss."

A breath caught in my throat. "Well, technically, it was over there." I gestured loosely to the tall oak, its branches clacking in the winter wind. Or maybe he was referring to the gazebo.

Ted gently pressed our clasped hands to his chest. "I remember exactly where we were. I remember everything about that day."

My cheeks heated, and my gaze drifted over his shoulder to where Cookie and Big Ed were chatting with a young family who had come to enjoy the rink on a beautiful Christmas day.

I do too.

We were sixteen. And for one perfect day, I wasn't just the nerdy kid who lived for extra credit. I was worth noticing. A handsome townie thought I was cute, fun, worth spending an entire day with. I hadn't reinvented myself; I'd just allowed myself to be someone who wasn't shaped by everyone else's expectations. That summer afternoon in this very park felt like a dream.

I glanced up at him, my heart pounding. "That was a long time ago."

His smile softened, and his brow arched subtly. "A lifetime."

The air between us crackled, thick with something unspoken.

"Do we need to wait another?" His easy teasing was gone now.

Wait another lifetime? I let out a slow breath. "I have a job. You have your life here. It's not that simple."

"It is, though." His voice was quiet but firm. "We make time. We figure it out. I don't care if it isn't ideal, Emily. I just care that it's you."

My throat tightened, and a rush of adrenaline made me hot under my thick coat. "You make it sound so easy." I found myself rephrasing the same argument because I didn't have another one.

"When have you ever taken the easy path?"

Goodness, how did he do that? How did he calm the chaos in my head? Make the impossible seem possible? I glanced away. "There's too much at stake. What if this attraction only works because we know it's temporary? What if this is a colossal mistake?"

"You don't believe that," he whispered, his voice rugged. He was calling my bluff.

Before I could react, he pulled me even closer. I instinctively clutched his jacket when my skate caught a rough patch.

"I got you," he murmured in my ear, making my breath hitch. He was so close, his warmth cutting through the cold. "Look at me." He gently hooked his gloved finger under my chin, giving me no choice. His eyes were warm, filled with something solid. Something sure. "This isn't a mistake."

My heart squeezed. I wanted to believe him.

I do believe him.

And so, for the first time in a long time, I stopped obsessing about making the right choice and simply leaned into what felt right. This felt right. *He* felt right.

Ted's fingers gently skimmed across my cheek. We locked gazes, time suspending before he brushed the lightest kiss across my cheek. His breath made goose bumps race along my skin when he whispered, "Don't worry about it, Emily. We'll figure it out."

All the walls I had built around my heart came tumbling down. I pulled back, searching his face, and in that moment, I knew we would.

His voice dropped, rough and low. "Can I kiss you?" A pause. "I know how you are about PDA."

I nodded, forgetting entirely about our nearby family. That was all the permission Ted needed. His lips met mine, cold at first, then blazing hot, sending a shockwave through my whole body. I bit back a groan. Why had I been resisting this? Why had I been resisting him?

After what seemed like forever and no time at all, we broke apart, and the world came rushing back in. Was that cheering? Someone wolf-whistled and called, "It's about time!" I would have placed my money on Cookie.

I whirled around to face our families, leaning back against Ted's solid chest and laughing. The four of them were looking on with glee, as if we were some sort of Christmas show on ice.

"What are we going to tell them?" The outside world, my plans, my carefully constructed future whispered at the edges of my mind. Was I still moving to Pittsburgh tomorrow? Starting that job? How would a long-distance thing work?

Ted wrapped his arms around me from behind, his chin resting on my shoulder, grounding me in the here and now. "Deep breath. We'll figure it out. Together."

epilogue/emily

Eight *Months Later*

I scanned the area, searching for a parking spot near the park. I had trays of desserts stacked in the back of my car. I had traded my sedan in for a more practical model. Sammie was manning the bakery booth for the end-of-summer carnival.

The same carnival where I'd spent that unforgettable summer day all those years ago. Nostalgia weighed heavy on my chest as I slowed, still searching for a parking spot amid the crowd. Most of the town seemed to be here, drawn out by the blue skies and soft breeze. It was the kind of perfect August day that made Cookie sigh and proclaim there was no better place to live in the summertime than Walleye Point.

Unsurprisingly, a couple of blocks down, the bakery and the brewery still competed for parking, though now it was a friendly competition where customers bounced between both businesses, grabbing lunch and a beer before heading to the bakery for coffee and something sweet. Or vice versa. Both businesses had an uptick of customers since the prize billboard went up on the New York State Thruway. It really was a win-win.

Just as I spotted a truck's taillights glowing red, my display indicated I had a call. "Dylan," I said with a grin as I answered. "You have a sixth sense for calling when I'm behind the wheel."

"I figured you'd be milking cows or bailing hay or whatever it is you folks do when you're in the country," he said, deadpan, clearly proud of his little joke.

"Okay, city boy. I'll have you know there are zero cows involved in my day." I backed up a bit to give the truck room to pull out. "How are you? How's that adorable baby of yours?"

"She's debating me in full sentences and rejecting classic rock in favor of bubblegum pop," he said with a weary fondness. "It's chaos. How's your life going?"

"Good. Busy." I eased the car into the space, excited to have found a spot close to where the bakery had a booth.

"I've heard."

I missed sharing the day-to-day details of my life with him. "Sorry I didn't get back to you last time you called," I said.

"No, I get it, life gets busy."

"Listen, I hate to do this to you, but I'm dropping off some desserts at the carnival," I said, turning off the ignition. "You and the family should come up sometime. I think you'd be impressed by our little town." *My little town.*

"That'd be nice," Dylan said, his voice softening. "Just wanted to check in. Call me when you're not delivering pastries or running the world."

"Will do. And give that fierce little girl a hug for me." I hung up, my smile lingering, and opened the car door and went around back to the open hatch.

A deep, gruff voice rang out. "I don't think you can park there, ma'am."

Furrowing my brow, I turned around, ready to ignore whatever grumpy Gus had opinions about parking. Until I saw him.

Ted.

Would my skin ever stop flushing and my heart stop racing when I saw him? Impossible. I couldn't believe I almost threw this all away because I didn't trust we could make a long-distance relationship work.

"Ha ha." I leaned in to slide the trays closer. "Just in time to help me carry these to the booth."

Ted kissed me in greeting, his hand sliding to the small of my back and pulling me flush against him. I let myself get lost in the pure bliss of knowing he was mine. When he deepened the kiss, I pressed a hand against his broad chest. "Easy, we're in public."

Ted made a show of glancing around but didn't let go. "No one's paying attention."

I gave him another quick kiss only to hear someone yell, "Gross. Get a room!"

My face burned hot, and I pulled away for real this time. Maddie and Jayden were jogging toward the car, Maddie clearly the culprit behind the teasing.

"Mom told me you might need help," she said.

I dipped my head, trying to shake the embarrassment, only to have Ted playfully tap my bum. I ignored him. Jayden grabbed one tray from the open trunk and Maddie another.

"How are sales going?" Ted asked.

"Fantastic. We can't keep Cookie's shortbread in stock," Maddie said. "Second most popular are the mini cinnamon buns." My niece's concoction. The bakery had become a real family affair. Maddie worked after school when she didn't have activities and had even expanded into the kitchen, testing new recipes.

"Aren't the apple tarts selling?" I asked, feeling a twinge of that competitiveness that was ingrained in me.

"Those are also popular," Jayden said. "We can't keep *anything* in stock."

Jayden and Maddie strode back to the booth, weighed down by the trays. They had started dating after the spring formal. Their relationship seemed easy and playful, perhaps what mine and Ted's could have been all those years ago if I hadn't been here only for the summer.

Who knew? I was just glad our paths eventually came together again, even if we had to wait years.

Too many years.

Ted grabbed a box of supplies from my trunk, and I grabbed the last tray of desserts and followed him toward the booth. We maneuvered our way through the crowd. When we reached the booth, a familiar sense of pride swelled in my chest.

For seventy-plus years, Cookie's bakery had proudly served sweet treats under a simple sign that read "Bakery." Now, the booth sported a whimsical new sign, matching the one above the store, that read "Knead Coffee?"

The winning name came after a laughter-filled night of board games and sugary snacks when Maddie yelled it out then immediately went to her notebook and drew up a mock design that ultimately came to life. It was perfect. The bakery was evolving, refashioning itself as a coffeehouse with fantastic baked goods.

Sammie rushed out from behind the booth, one hand instinctively resting on her belly. "Just in time! Everyone's asking for the shortbread." Cookie's shortbread had become so popular, they were now selling it online, making a tidy profit.

Sammie tried to grab the tray from Maddie, but her daughter pivoted away. "I got it." Maddie balanced the tray's edge against the counter while Sammie slipped on a glove to refill the baskets.

Trevor ran over with a replacement case of water, a big

grin on his face. He twisted the cap off a bottle and handed it to his wife. "Here. Sit."

I watched the scene, warmth spreading through me. Trevor had been doting on his wife from the minute she'd announced she was having another baby. My second niece or nephew would be seventeen years younger than my first one.

And this time, I wouldn't miss any of it.

Ted reached around my middle and pressed a chaste kiss to my cheek. "What are you smiling about?"

I sighed, contentment sinking into my bones. "I'm happy."

For so long, I had measured success by my career, tying my worth to my achievements. But peace came from within, not from what I accomplished.

After two months of trying to work in Pittsburgh and maintain a long-distance relationship, I'd made the decision to move to Walleye Point permanently.

As soon as I did, the weight of the world lifted from me.

Ted had encouraged me to stick with Blue Moon Investment Group, told me he didn't mind traveling to see me, but his unwavering support had made it easier to leave what I thought was my future.

Now, I worked part-time in the bakery, and I'd started a nonprofit helping women become financially savvy. Like I said, I'd never been happier.

A few feet away from me, Cookie stood and her chair dipped on the uneven lawn, sending her off balance. I was closest and reached her first. "You okay?"

My grandmother laughed. "The leg of the chair sank into the grass."

Once I was sure she was steady, I stepped back, but she held onto my arm, her eyes twinkling. "If you two hurry up, maybe you can have a baby the same age as her cousin."

"Cookie!" I feigned shock, but the idea had crossed my mind. I'd have to wait for the ring, though. There were some things I was old-fashioned about.

Big Ed said from his chair in the shade, "My boy needs to hurry it up."

At that, Ted cocked an eyebrow then shook his head. "I don't need you, old man, to tell me how it is."

Big Ed smirked. "Never did."

Ted reached down and took my hand. "Come here."

We weaved through the crowd to the gazebo. Flowers that hadn't been there earlier today adorned the railing. Mrs. Davis, the florist, stood nearby, hands clasped, clearly pleased with herself. I greeted her quickly, and she smiled. We had reconnected over the past few months, and she reassured me that life after the floral shop was fantastic. "Coming out of retirement for the day was worth it," she said, making me wonder what was going on exactly. "You've got yourself a good man."

I spun back around and locked into Ted. My brain swirled as he stepped up onto the gazebo, pulling me behind him. A rush of anticipation made my mouth go dry.

He turned to face me. "I was going to do this during the fireworks tonight, but you'd expect that." He slid a hand into his pocket, pulled out a ring, and dropped to one knee.

My hands pressed to my chest. My heart pounded.

"Emily Johnson," he said, his voice cracking, "will you do me the honor of becoming my wife?"

Tears blurred my vision. I bent down and kissed him, sealing my answer without words.

The crowd roared.

We had our forever.

And this time, we weren't racing against summer.

This time, we had all the time in the world.

———

Dear Reader,

Thank you for choosing **ALL I KNEAD FOR**

CHRISTMAS and spending time in Walleye Point. Bringing Emily and Ted's story to life—from their snowy "meet-cute" to that pivotal moment at the carnival gazebo—was a lot of fun. Emily's dedication to both her finance career and family, alongside Ted's commitment to his brewery and nephew Jayden, reminds us that second chances at love are always possible.

If light, closed-door romantic comedies are your jam, I have wonderful news:

There's more to discover in Walleye Point!

ALL I KNEAD FOR CHRISTMAS is actually the third standalone in this series. Begin where it all started with:

- **A FINE MESS** (Book 1)

- **CACHE ME IF YOU CAN** (Book 2)

Each story stands on its own while sharing the same beloved setting and a few familiar faces. Already read all three? Visit my "Also By" page for more heartwarming stories.

Your readership means everything to me.

Warmly,

Alison Stone

about the author

Alison Stone is the author of witty romantic comedies. She grew up in Buffalo, NY, as the fourth of five kids, where having a sense of humor was a matter of survival. She writes romances full of emotion that evoke the warm and fuzzies, and she prefers to keep the hanky-panky behind closed doors.

Alison also writes clean and wholesome small-town romantic suspense, some of which have bonnets and buggies.

Check out her "Also by" page for more reading suggestions.

also by alison stone

The Thrill of Sweet Suspense Series

(Stand-alone novels that can be read in any order)

Random Acts

Too Close to Home

Critical Diagnosis

Grave Danger

The Art of Deception

Hunters Ridge: Amish Romantic Suspense

The Millionaire's Amish Bride: Hunters Ridge Amish Romance

Plain Obsession: Book 1

Plain Missing: Book 2

Plain Escape: Book 3

Plain Revenge: Book 4

Plain Survival: Book 5

Plain Inferno: Book 6

Plain Trouble: Book 7

Plain Secrets: Book 8

A Jayne Murphy Dance Academy Cozy Mystery

Pointe & Shoot

Final Curtain

Corpse de Ballet

9 781964 598109